# The Summer Riders

Also by Patricia Leitch and published by Catnip:

For Love of a Horse
A Devil to Ride

# The Summer Riders

## Patricia Leitch

CATNIP BOOKS
Published by Catnip Publishing Ltd
14 Greville Street
London
EC1N 8SB

This edition first published 2010

1 3 5 7 9 10 8 6 4 2

Text copyright © Patricia Leitch, 1977
The moral right of the author has been asserted.

Cover design by Chris Fraser
Cover photography by Karen Budkiewicz

A CIP catalogue record for this book is available from the British Library.

ISBN 978-1-84647-112-4

Printed in Poland

www.catnippublishing.co.uk

# FOREWORD
## by Lauren St John, author of *The White Giraffe*

*For Love of a Horse*, the first book in the *Jinny at Finmory* series, is my favourite pony book of all time. I read it for the first time when I was about eleven and every bit as horse mad as Jinny, and it's hard to overstate how much impact it had on me and how much I related to the story and to Jinny's relationship with her horse. It didn't matter that Jinny lived at Finmory on the Scottish moors and spent her days passionately trying to save or tame a chestnut Arab mare, and I lived on a remote farm in Africa and spent my days trying to save and train a black stallion, it seemed to me that the way we thought, felt and dreamed about the horses we loved was identical.

Imagine having a best friend who thinks about riding exactly the way you do; who gets into the same kind of disastrous, scary or embarrassing situations and suffers the same kind of highs and lows, and who just happens to have the horse of your dreams. That's what Jinny and Shantih were for me. Over the years, scores of other fans of the series have felt the same way. You will too. And if you're anything like me, you'll be drawing pictures of Shantih and pinning them up on your bedroom wall, reading each book at least five times, and wishing and dreaming that you had a chestnut Arab mare just like Shantih and could gallop across the moors with Jinny, mysterious, magical Ken, and all the other characters who make up Jinny's world at Finmory.

You're in for the ride of your life. Enjoy!

Lauren St John
*London, 2010*

# *One*

Jinny Manders woke with the thought quite clear in her mind that today was the first day of the summer holidays.

'The summer holidays,' Jinny said aloud and shivered with excitement.

She jumped out of bed and padded on bare feet across her bedroom to the window that looked out to the rolling hills and high, rocky crags that surrounded Finmory House. Nothing stirred in the grey summer dawn. Then, as Jinny stared out, the glistening golden disc of the sun began to slip up from behind the hills. The high, cloudless sky shimmered into blue.

*Going to be a brilliant day*, thought Jinny. *I'll go for a ride now,* she decided. *Before anyone else is awake. Nobody to spoil it. Just Shantih and me.*

Jinny somersaulted back across her room, past the

mural of a red horse charging through a jungle of white flowers, past her own drawings and paintings pinned to the walls, under the arch that separated the two halves of her room and did a floppy cartwheel over her bed to reach her other window. It faced in the opposite direction, looked over Finmory's garden, down to the ponies' field and on to Finmory Bay and the glittering reach of the sea.

Jinny opened the window wide and leaned out, her long, red-gold hair swinging over the sill.

'Shantih,' Jinny called. 'Shantih.'

Punch and Bramble, the two borrowed trekking ponies that Jinny and her younger brother Mike had ridden to school, went on grazing, ignoring her, but the third horse looked up, instantly alert at the sound of Jinny's voice.

'Shantih,' Jinny breathed, and the Arab horse whinnied in reply, her nostrils dark pits in her delicate, dished face. Her ears were pricked above her silken forelock and her dark, lustrous eyes looked up at Jinny from under long-fringed lashes. She was a pure-bred Arab, red-gold with a white blaze and four white socks, and Jinny loved her completely, totally.

Jinny had first seen Shantih in a circus. Then she had been "Yasmin, the Killer Horse", being lashed into rearing viciousness by the ringmaster. But now she belonged to Jinny and was Shantih, which means peace. Ken had chosen the name, saying that names changed people and that it would help Shantih to forget the circus.

Almost a year ago, Jinny and her family – Petra who was now fifteen and Mike who was ten – had all left the city life of Stopton, where Mr Manders had been a probation officer, to come and live at Finmory House. It was a large, grey, stone house in the Scottish Highlands. Their nearest neighbour was Mr MacKenzie, whose farm supplied the Manders with milk and eggs, and then there was nothing but moorland until the tiny village of Glenbost where Mike and Jinny went to school. Now Mr Manders made his living as a potter, helped by Ken, who was seventeen and was staying with the Manders.

They had first got to know Ken Dawson when he had been on probation in Stopton, charged with other boys for breaking into a warehouse. At the end of his probation he had said to Mr Manders, 'I'd nothing to do with it.' 'I know,' Mr Manders had acknowledged.

Although Ken's parents were rich enough to send him a monthly cheque, they wanted nothing further to do with him. 'Just so long as they know I'm not starving,' Ken had mocked when his first cheque had arrived direct from the bank, and he had laughed, stuffing it into the pocket of his jeans. But Jinny hadn't thought it was funny. Your own parents not loving you. She couldn't even bear to think it might be possible.

'We want you here,' she had assured Ken. 'I care.' And Ken had smiled directly at her, his green eyes bright in his thin, tanned face. He had pushed back his long, straw-coloured hair and looked down at her from his bony height. 'Thank you,' he'd said and gone out to the vegetable garden he was creating, with Kelly, his grey, shaggy dog padding at his heels.

Jinny wasn't quite sure what was the best thing, Ken living with them or owning Shantih. She could never make up her mind.

Shantih whinnied again and walked towards the hedge closest to the house, her stride neat and precise through the dew-dark grass.

'We're going for a ride,' Jinny told her. 'I shan't be long. Stay there.'

A few minutes later Jinny was flipping down the steep flight of stairs that led from her attic bedroom. She ran along the corridor, down the wide staircase to the hall and into the kitchen. She was the first, there was no one else awake. She paused for a second to choose two apples, one for herself and one for Shantih, then she opened the heavy back door, hearing its creaking echoing through the sleeping house, and she was free. In the back yard she whirled round and round, her long hair flying out about her skinny body.

'Summer,' she yelled. 'Summer, summer, summer.' And thought of galloping over the moors, swimming Shantih in the sea, camping by Loch Varrich – if she could find a tent. Days and days of being with Shantih. 'And it was summer; warm delightful summer,' said Jinny slowly.

The Manders' stables had once been crumbling outhouses. Now there was a place for tack and the horses' feed, two stalls for the Highland ponies and a loose box for Shantih. Jinny took down Shantih's snaffle bridle. Beside it, polished and gleaming, was the tack belonging to Bramble and Punch. Jinny swallowed hard and tried not to look at it. It wasn't that she had forgotten that tomorrow Punch and Bramble were going back to Miss Tuke's trekking centre, just that she wasn't allowing it to come up to the surface of her mind. Tomorrow would be time enough to think about Shantih being alone in the field and Miss Tuke taking back both saddles which meant that Jinny would need to ride bareback all the time. Jinny didn't mind riding bareback but she had to admit that without a saddle Shantih would be able to throw her off more often than usual.

*Nobody, absolutely nobody, could possibly say that Shantih wasn't improving*, Jinny thought. Only this Easter Jinny had spent most of her rides flying through the air while Shantih bucked or reared, but now she managed to stay on top most of the time.

Jinny counted on her fingers as she walked down to the ponies' field. Last week she had only been bucked off six times and Shantih hadn't really reared at all.

Not what you'd call rearing. There had been rather a nasty moment when they had met Mr MacKenzie's tractor, but she hadn't actually reared, Jinny decided, just tipped up a bit, and it had all been Mr MacKenzie's fault, coming charging round the corner when he knew he might meet them.

*He does it for kicks*, thought Jinny darkly. *Lurks and pounces on us.*

Shantih was waiting at the field gate and whickered when she saw Jinny.

'Horse,' said Jinny lovingly, 'are you in a good mood or can you smell the apples?'

Jinny slipped the bridle over the Arab's head and led her out of the field. She shared the apples with her, feeling Shantih's velvet muzzle lipping her hand.

'Finished,' Jinny told her. 'That's all.' Shantih pushed at Jinny to make sure. 'Come on,' said Jinny. 'We're going down to the sea.'

Jinny sprang up onto Shantih's back. There hadn't seemed much point in dirtying a saddle for one day, not after Mike had helped her to clean the tack. Now that Punch and Bramble were going back to Miss Tuke's trekking centre Jinny didn't suppose she'd be seeing much of her brother round the stables. Mike was easy-going and cheerful, with brown eyes and curly hair. Jinny liked being with him but she knew that although Mike was fond of Punch he wouldn't really mind not having a pony to ride. Mike's summer holidays would be full of his own things – fishing and helping Alec Clark on his father's farm, hoping that he might just be allowed to drive the tractor.

Petra was even less horsy than Mike. When it suited her she didn't mind sitting sweetly on a horse with a headscarf knotted at just the right angle over her curls, but most of the time Petra wasn't in the least interested in Shantih. Really, Jinny was quite glad. Whenever Petra was around, Jinny seemed to make more of a muddle of things than usual. Sometimes Jinny thought that her sister was made up of all the opposites to herself. She was sharp and efficient and organised; her curly hair was always tidy and her clothes always looked clean and smart.

*And bossy*, thought Jinny. *Very bossy indeed*. Later in the summer Petra was going to sit an important music exam and all her spare time would be spent practising the piano. Jinny knew she would pass. Passing exams was one of Petra's things. Reading teenage fashion magazines was another. *But not helping me with Shantih*, Jinny decided.

It wasn't that Jinny wanted anyone else to ride Shantih but she couldn't help thinking that it would be nice to have a friend. Someone to ride with her. None of the other children at the village school was the least interested in ponies. They thought of them as things they had kept around the crofts before the tractors came.

*What I would like,'* thought Jinny, *is another girl who has her own pony and knows a bit about schooling. Someone who could tell me what I'm doing wrong. Someone to help me to lunge her* . . . Jinny stopped in mid-thought. During the Easter holidays she had tried to make Clare Burnley help her with Shantih and things had gone disastrously wrong. It was not something that Jinny allowed herself to think about too often.

'All past. Utterly past,' said Jinny, and she gathered up Shantih's reins and urged her into a canter. Shantih bucked. Jinny sailed over her head, landed on her feet and sprang back up, almost in one smooth circle.

'Get on with you,' shouted Jinny, sitting tight and close. 'On you go.' And the mare was cantering smoothly towards the beach. The sea breeze flicked back her mane and lifted strands of Jinny's red hair. Jinny laid the palm of her hand flat on Shantih's shoulder, feeling the power of the Arab's stride.

'Faster,' urged Jinny and the mare stretched her neck and raced over the rough grass.

Jinny brought Shantih back to a walk before they reached the beach. She slowed down reluctantly, snaking her head and jangling her bit, curtseying suddenly sideways, her tail kinked over her back.

'Don't bother showing off,' said Jinny severely. 'There's no one to see you. Walk now. Steady.'

Shantih strode down the path between the massed

boulders and out into the dazzle of the shore. On the sands Jinny stopped her and sat staring over the water. Gulls searching for an early breakfast looped the sky or squabbled at the edge of the surf; a pied squadron of oyster catchers flew low over the sea.

*Amazing*! thought Jinny, glutted with the blue and silver and gold. 'Just think, you might still have been in your piggy circus and I might have been stuck in filthy old Stopton. You remember, Shantih Manders, how lucky you are and stop bucking me off.'

Shantih flickered disinterested ears and dug impatiently at the wet sand until Jinny let her walk on along the beach.

At the far side of the bay, on the grass above the barrier of sea-smoothed boulders, was something that looked to Jinny like a bright yellow sheet hanging out to dry. She peered at it but couldn't make out what it could be, then trotted Shantih towards it, thinking that it might be some sort of shelter that Mr MacKenzie had put up. Then suddenly she stopped Shantih and stared in disbelief at the sands in front of her.

*It can't be!* thought Jinny. *Yet it is!*

Someone, but Jinny couldn't imagine who it could possibly have been, had been schooling a horse. The wet sand was pitted with hoofprints. Circles, figure eights and serpentines were tracked out on the sand. For a moment Jinny wondered if Clare Burnley might have been riding on the shore but Jinny knew the

Burnleys were still in Sussex and their house, Craigvaar, was still empty. And it couldn't have been Mike or Petra or Ken. Even if one of them had taken a Highland for a ride they would never ever have brought him down here to school.

*Man Friday*, thought Jinny, and jumped down to examine the marks more closely.

They were certainly hoofprints. Someone had been schooling a horse there and not so very long ago. Then suddenly Shantih jerked her head into the air, almost snatching the reins out of Jinny's hand. She whinnied with a blast of sound and was answered with a high, squealing neigh. Almost invisible against the boulders a girl in jodphurs and a yellow tee shirt was riding a skewbald pony.

Jinny threw herself back up onto Shantih, knowing that if the Arab got too excited she might not be able to get up onto her again. With neck arched and tail high, Shantih pranced across the sands towards the skewbald. The girl had seen them. She waved and walked her pony to meet them.

The brown and white pony was thick-set and cobby, with a shaving brush mane and a placid, two-colour expression. His rider looked about twelve years old, about the same age as Jinny. She had short, brown, wavy hair, a tip-tilted nose and wide-set, hazel eyes. She wasn't fat, but rather like her pony, Jinny thought, sturdy and reliable-looking.

They were within a few yards of the girl and her skewbald when Shantih reared violently, hung poised in the air, balanced on her hind legs. Jinny clung round her neck helplessly until she touched down again.

'It's the strange pony . . .' Jinny began, her face scarlet from being scrubbed into Shantih's mane. She looked defiantly across at the girl, expecting to see her laughing at Shantih's bad manners and Jinny's rotten riding, but on the girl's round, freckled face was an expression of total admiration.

'She is absolutely super,' said the girl. 'She's an Arab, isn't she? Is she yours? I've always wanted an Arab. And a chestnut too! Oh, she is beautiful!'

Jinny's sharp features spread into an ear-to-ear grin. It wasn't often she met someone who said the things that she herself thought about Shantih.

'Super horse,' repeated the girl, still gazing at Shantih. 'Oh, how I'd love a horse like that.'

'She gets a bit excited,' apologised Jinny. 'She used to be in a circus where they treated her badly.'

'Not that I don't think Pippen is the mostest pony and wouldn't change him for anything. But an Arab . . .'

'I'm Jinny Manders,' said Jinny. 'And this is Shantih. We live at Finmory House.'

'You don't! We saw it last night when we arrived. Dad said he'd give anything to live there but Mum said there'd be mice. I'm Sue, Sue Horton, and this is Pippen.'

'Are you staying here?' asked Jinny.

'Camping,' said Sue. 'All summer. Normally we have a fortnight in a stuffy hotel but with things being so expensive we bought a tent and more or less at the last minute we were able to borrow a trailer and bring Pippen with us. Thought we were going to have to leave you behind all summer, didn't we?' said Sue, ruffling the skewbald's mane. 'Would you look at it?' she said. 'Every spring I swear I'm going to let it grow and it goes on growing up and up and up. Then every autumn I give in and have it clipped again. Still, perhaps this time . . .' She grinned, then said, 'You are lucky living here. Can you ride all over the hills?'

'More or less,' said Jinny. 'You have to watch out for boggy bits on the moors but there are lots of places where it's quite safe to gallop.'

'Shall we go for a ride together?' asked Sue. 'That's if you'd like to. I don't want to be tagging on.'

'Like to!' exclaimed Jinny. 'Honestly I was longing for someone to ride with. I'm the only one who's keen on horses in my family.'

'Well, I'm the only anything one,' said Sue.

'This morning?' asked Jinny. 'We could go for a ride this morning if you like.'

'Not at all today,' said Sue regretfully. 'We're all going to Inverburgh to stock up and Dad wants some new fishing gear – but every day after that.'

'Sue! Sue! Breakfast's ready,' called a voice, and

Jinny, seeing a woman standing by the bright yellow sheet, realised that it was part of an elaborate tent.

'How about tomorrow?' Sue asked.

'This time,' said Jinny. 'Very early.' And then she explained about having to return Punch and Bramble to Miss Tuke.

'See you here, then. Tomorrow at seven.'

'Right,' said Jinny, sitting very tight on Shantih in case she reared again when Sue rode Pippen away. 'Bye.'

Riding back to Finmory, squeaks of delight burst out of Jinny.

'And a friend for you,' she told Shantih. 'Dare say Pippen can share your field. Will that be nice?'

Jinny's family were all sitting round the kitchen table having breakfast when Jinny burst into the kitchen.

'There's a family camping on the beach,' Jinny told them. 'And there's a girl called Sue, 'bout my age I should think, *and she's got a pony*!'

'Oh, I'm glad,' said Mrs Manders. 'She'll be company for you. I've been worrying about you riding Shantih by yourself all summer.'

'Well, you don't need to now,' said Jinny. 'I'll be riding with Sue.' All the things Jinny had been planning to do were suddenly warmer, more exciting, now that they were to be shared with someone else. 'We're going for a ride tomorrow.'

'What about the sad returning?' asked Mike.

'Hadn't forgotten,' said Jinny, making herself toast. 'We're going to ride early.'

'The Thorpes come tomorrow,' said her father.

'Tomorrow!' cried Jinny. 'But I thought they weren't coming until the end of August!'

'That was changed weeks ago,' said Petra, crimping at her crispbread with her front teeth. 'You never listen to anything, do you?'

'When was it changed? No one told me,' said Jinny indignantly.

The Thorpes were two children Mr Manders had known in Stopton. The boy, Bill Thorpe, was thirteen and had been on probation for shoplifting. Since the Manders had been at Finmory, Bill had spent six months in hospital with lung trouble. Mr Manders had heard from a colleague that they were trying to get Bill away from Stopton for a holiday in the country but were having trouble fixing it up because the boy's younger sister wanted to go with him. 'Send them to us,' Mr Manders had offered, and the visit had been arranged.

'Well, everyone else knew,' said Mike.

'I didn't. And I think someone could have told me,' grumphed Jinny, sitting down beside her father with her plate of blackish toast. The very last thing she wanted was two unknown Stopton children coming to stay just when she had found a friend. Jinny hacked at the butter and spread it thickly on her toast. She gulped the coffee that her mother had poured out for her.

'Having a tiny tantrum, are we?' asked Petra.

'Well . . . I didn't know they were coming,' said Jinny. 'Still, I don't suppose I'll see much of them. I'll be riding Shantih with Sue.'

Ken got up from the table, pushing his chair back with a sharp sound of disgust. He went silently out of the back door, his bony shoulders hunched.

Jinny ignored his departure.

'What's the sister's name?' Mike asked.

'Marlene,' said Mr Manders. 'She's ten. Both lived in Stopton all their lives.'

'Hasn't the girl got a bad leg?' asked his wife.

'A bad leg?' said Jinny. 'Then she won't want to ride, will she?'

'She was knocked down crossing the road when she was about six,' said her father. 'Her leg was badly broken and never set properly. Now she walks with a severe limp.' Mr Manders went to get a sheet of paper out of his desk.

'Meant to show you this,' he said to Jinny, handing it to her. 'Marlene's teacher gave it to Tim Lawrence, the social worker who's working with the Thorpes. I must have mentioned Shantih to him and he must have told Marlene about her. Anyway this is what she wrote. Normally her compositions consist of one or two words. Read it.'

Jinny looked suspiciously at the folded page that

had obviously been taken from a school exercise book. She took it from her father unwillingly. The writing was uneven and sprawling and even Jinny could see that the spelling was terrible.

This sumer I am to ride a arab hors. We will gallopp. When I am on the hors you wont see me leg is wonky. It wont mattar. I think the hors will be ok with me. He is spesull. I will lov the hors. When I am on the hors we will go fast as flames.

When Jinny had finished reading she kept her eyes on the paper. The girl must be daft thinking she could come and gallop Shantih. No one who hadn't been on a horse before could just get on a horse and gallop off.

'She could have had a ride on Bramble if he hadn't had to go back to Miss Tuke,' Jinny muttered. 'Or perhaps Sue would let her have a ride on her pony. He looked pretty quiet. But not on Shantih.'

Mr Manders took back Marlene's composition.

'I think the hors will be ok with me,' he read.

'Well, I don't think Shantih will be OK with her,' stated Jinny. 'She can't ride. She can't arrive here and expect to go galloping off on Shantih.'

'Fast as flames,' said her father.

'Not fast as flames on my horse,' muttered Jinny sullenly.

# *Two*

The next morning Shantih and Jinny careered down the track to the beach. Jinny had slept in and was still feeling cross and gritty. Shantih, catching her irritation, was playing up. She would bound forward then jerk to a sudden halt, wait with her neck arched and every muscle tensed – totally ignoring her rider, who was perched insecurely on her bare back – then with a half rear she would spin round and plunge back to her field.

'Oh, come on then,' said Jinny furiously, when she had been carted back to Punch and Bramble three times. 'I'll just have to lead you or Sue will be back in her tent.'

Jinny dragged the reins over Shantih's head and, tugging on her bit, set off for the beach.

'Might as well be pulling a rhinoceros,' muttered Jinny as she plodded towards the sea. Her book on horsemanship said that you should never look back when you were leading a horse. ''Spect she has changed,' Jinny decided. 'Wonder what Sue will say. Expect she'll be polite. "What strange horns your horse has got," she'll say, and I'll say, "All the better to charge you with".'

From the direction of the beach came a shrill whinny. Shantih froze, her eyes goggling. Just in time, Jinny lassoed the reins over her head and managed to scrabble onto her back before Shantih, with an answering whinny, was galloping down the track.

Jinny fell off when Shantih executed a four-hoof emergency stop in front of Pippen and Sue.

'Hi,' said Sue as Jinny picked herself up off the sand. 'She looked fantastic galloping like that.'

'Huh,' grunted Jinny. 'She wouldn't leave the Highlands. That's why I'm so late. She must have known they're going away today.'

'I've been schooling him,' said Sue. 'Would you watch for a minute and see if he does change legs when we do a figure eight?'

'I'll try,' said Jinny, who wasn't too sure what it looked like when a horse did change legs, although she knew it was the correct thing to do.

Watching Pippen cantering round, Jinny grinned to herself as she imagined his legs dropping off and reassembling themselves at the centre of the figure eight.

'No good, was it?' demanded Sue when she rode back to Jinny. 'He trotted.'

Jinny thought it best to agree.

'Would you mind if we stayed here and schooled? It's after eight so we haven't much time for a ride.'

Jinny didn't think Shantih was in the mood for schooling but she had promised Mike that she would be ready to set off for Miss Tuke's before ten.

'Even leaving at ten we won't get there much before twelve,' Mike had said. 'Dad's meeting us there with the car. We've to take his pots in to Miss Storr's shop and then be at the station to meet the two-thirty train. You be late to start with and the whole day will be a mess.'

'That's right,' Jinny had replied. 'Make it all my fault. And we haven't even begun.'

But Jinny knew that if they went for a ride now she wouldn't be ready to set out at ten and it would be her fault.

*Flippin' time*, thought Jinny, already seeing how the day was going to be full of people telling her to hurry up.

'Well, all right,' she said to Sue, 'but Shantih isn't very good at schooling.'

'Walk her round in a circle,' suggested Sue and Jinny rode Shantih out in a wide circle.

It took all Jinny's concentration to keep Shantih going round at a walk, and each time they passed Sue and Pippen the circle bulged towards them.

'Try a trot,' called Sue.

'Well . . .' said Jinny, but she closed her fingers on Shantih's reins, tightening her legs against the Arab's sides.

Shantih leapt forward into a raking trot and there was a moment when Jinny felt all the pride and gaiety of her horse as she flowed round the circle, but the next minute Shantih was fighting to get to Pippen. Jinny shortened her left rein and kicked with her right heel.

'Get on,' she shouted. 'Get on with you,' as Shantih began to buck, her head tucked between her forelegs, her quarters and hind legs soaring skywards. Clinging to a lump of hairy wither, Jinny clamped her knees against Shantih's hard shoulders and fought to stay on. Sue was shouting to her but Jinny couldn't hear her, could only see her mouth opening and shutting and Pippen's bland, brown and white face as he knitted his brows in disapproval at such behaviour.

Shantih managed to work a twist into her fourth buck that sent Jinny sprawling towards her ears. Arms linked round her mare's neck, Jinny slithered to the ground.

'Gosh,' said Sue. 'Is that what she did in the circus?'

'She is much, much better than she used to be,' stated Jinny firmly. 'She didn't feel like schooling. It was my fault. I should have known better. She hardly ever mucks about when we go for a ride. I don't blame her for bucking. If I wanted to go over the moors and some stupid human tried to make me go round in circles I'd buck them off.' Jinny rubbed Shantih's neck and stroked her hand over her muzzle. 'She gets excited, that's all. I don't mind.'

'She looked terrific,' said Sue. 'All mane and tail and hooves. I'd be scared stiff to ride her. Bit of a coward, that's me.'

'Me too,' said Jinny in surprise that anyone should think of her as brave. 'Only it's different with Shantih.'

'You don't use a stick, do you?' asked Sue. 'Mrs Ross at our Pony Club would say that she needed to be taught a lesson.'

'Clare Burnley thought that too. But it's no use. The ringmaster at that circus whipped her. It only makes her go mad.'

'Well, I think I'd ride with a saddle.'

'Well I did,' said Jinny. 'Haven't got one now. I used one of the ponies' saddles but it goes back to Miss Tuke today.' And guiltily Jinny remembered about the time. Her watch said ten to twelve, which Jinny considered unlikely.

'But I can lend you one!' said Sue. 'I thought you were improving your seat. Come up to the tent and we'll see if it fits.'

'Oh, but I couldn't take that,' cried Jinny when Sue, after a car key sortie into the tent, unlocked the boot of their car and took out an almost brand-new saddle. 'It's far too good.'

'Try it on,' said Sue, ignoring Jinny's protests.

Sue fitted the saddle onto Shantih's back. 'There,' she said, tightening the girth. 'Seems perfect. Get up. I must look under it while you're sitting on it to make sure I can see daylight under the channel.

'Perfect,' said Sue, squinting under the saddle when Jinny was mounted. 'Not touching her spine.'

'But I can't just take it,' gasped Jinny. Her knees were tucked against the knee rolls and she sat with a new sense of security in the deep seat of the saddle. 'It's too good. I mean, you don't really know me. And it's such a splendid saddle.'

'Please borrow it,' said Sue. 'I'd be glad to see someone using it. Perhaps it will stop Dad moaning. My cousin, who is completely spoiled, thought she wanted to ride. They bought her everything, including a beastly show pony. Of course she fell off, broke her arm, and that was that. No more ponies. Screamed if she saw one. They had to sell the lot. I persuaded Dad to buy the saddle for Pippen. And he's too broad for it. 'Course I really knew that, didn't I, but I so wanted to have it. It gave Pippen a sore back and I can't use it. We brought it with us because Dad thinks this holiday will slim Pippen down. If it doesn't he's going to sell it. Now if you were using it you'd be doing me a favour. It upsets Dad when he sees it lying around.'

'He didn't buy it for me to use,' insisted Jinny. 'Perhaps seeing me using it would upset him more.' She couldn't believe that a more or less complete stranger was offering to lend her the kind of saddle that she had always dreamed about but known she could never afford.

A stoutish woman with long, dark hair came out of the tent.

'Mum,' called Sue. 'Here. This is Jinny who lives at Finmory House.'

The woman pulled a heavy sweater over her head and came towards them.

'Hullo,' she said, smiling with Sue's smile and holding her hand out to Jinny. 'Just crawled out of our burrow. Shocking lying in bed until this time on a camping holiday.'

'Time!' remembered Jinny.

'I'm lending Jinny the saddle,' said Sue.

'Grand,' said Mrs Horton. 'Glad to see someone using it. Gave poor old Pippen a bad back, didn't it, son? I'm about to brew up. Will you two have a cup?'

'Is it nine o'clock yet?' Jinny asked, wondering desperately if she could ride off with Sue's saddle; just turn round and ride off with a brand-new saddle or whether she should offer to sign some sort of agreement or even leave a deposit – not that she had any money.

'Twenty past,' Mrs Horton told her.

'Oh no,' cried Jinny. 'I'll need to go.'

'You will,' said Sue. 'I'd forgotten all about the time.'

'They'll be mad with me,' said Jinny, already

beginning to turn Shantih towards Finmory. 'Are you sure it's OK for me to take the saddle?'

'Certain,' said Mrs Horton.

'I told you,' said Sue.

'Well, thank you very much indeed,' said Jinny. 'I mean thank you isn't enough but I will need to go.'

'Then go,' said Sue, giggling. 'Don't keep telling us.'

'See you tomorrow,' Jinny shouted back as she cantered off. 'Come up to Finmory.'

Halfway across the field, Shantih's head went down and she began to buck.

'Ah, no you don't. Not this time.' And Jinny, bracing her knees against the knee rolls and sitting deep in the saddle, was able to pull Shantih's head up and send her on.

'This saddle,' Jinny told her horse as they cantered home, 'is going to make a great deal of difference in your life. See if it doesn't.' And she thought that she would do some drawings of Pippen and give them to Sue. As Jinny rode home she could see quite clearly how she would paint the skewbald pony. She knew the way his hooves had to be round and settled into the ground, his neck bulky and his ears thickly rooted into his head. She could feel how she would draw the corners of his smug lips. Jinny didn't understand how she knew these things. They came welling up inside her and then she was able to draw them.

The ponies' field was empty, and as Jinny took off

Shantih's tack and turned her loose, she supposed that Mike must have taken both Highlands to their stalls.

'You're late,' shouted Petra's voice.

'Surprise, surprise,' shouted back Jinny, running up to her bedroom and setting the new saddle carefully in a corner. She paused for a second of utter disbelief and then ran out to the stables.

'Thought you were going to be back before nine,' said Mike, who was grooming the white Punch. 'I've brought them in and given them a last feed. We don't want to arrive at Miss Tuke's with them covered in sweat. She'll think that's the way we've been treating them all year.'

'Well, we haven't,' said Jinny, grabbing a dandy and starting to groom Bramble. Under the strokes of the brush Bramble's summer coat gleamed like jet, dapples spangled his quarters and broad barrel. Jinny ran her hands down his flat knees and strong-boned legs. She brushed out his feathery fetlocks and tipped his haystack mane from one side of his neck to the other as she tried to brush it flat.

'I shall miss you terribly,' she whispered to the pony, remembering all the wild gallops they had shared, all the journeys to and from school. Jinny buried her face in Bramble's mane. She wanted to keep him, wanted to find her parents and try to persuade them to buy Bramble. Punch could go back to Miss Tuke's, but Bramble belonged to her.

'No time,' said Mike. 'Don't start to cry. You should have been earlier if you wanted to go on like that.'

Reluctantly Jinny supposed so. She put on Bramble's tack and went inside. Her mother caught her and made her drink a cup of coffee and gobble down a bacon sandwich.

All the family came to say goodbye to the ponies.

Ken, his hands encrusted with clay, held his face out to them and breathed in their nostrils. 'Been nice having you with us,' he murmured, rubbing his face against their fumbling lips.

'He'll be back in September,' said Petra, seeing her sister's red eyes. 'You'll still need him to take you into the village.'

Next term Jinny was to go to the new comprehensive school that was still being built in Inverburgh. She would ride Bramble into Glenbost, leave him there and catch a school bus. Jinny was sorry to be leaving the village school. Trailing in and out to Inverburgh every day wouldn't leave her much time for Shantih. But it was so much better than going with Petra to Duninver school where you had to spend the week in the school hostel that Jinny had hardly grumbled at all.

'But I don't want him to go,' said Jinny obstinately. 'Couldn't we keep Bramble, even if we have to pay for him? He would be just right for this Marlene to learn on.'

'I'll be at Miss Tuke's for half-past twelve,' Mr

Manders said, ignoring Jinny. 'We must be away from there before one if I'm to get my pottery delivered.'

'Oh, OK,' said Jinny. 'Don't go on about it. We're going.'

But they had to wait in the farmyard while Mr MacKenzie found a bit of turnip for the ponies, said they had been like hairy vacuum cleaners when it came to the oats and that it hadn't taken Jinny long to be scrounging her way down to the tent.

'Scotland Yard needs you,' said Jinny. In all the months she had known Mr MacKenzie she had never managed to discover how he managed to know about things almost before they happened.

By the time they had waited for the ponies to scrunch their way through the turnip they were even later.

'Come on,' said Mike, when they had escaped from the old farmer. 'We're not even going to be in time to meet Bill and Marlene at this rate.'

'Fuss, fuss, fuss,' said Jinny. 'You're growing up just like Petra,' but she urged Bramble on along the road to Glenbost.

They clattered through the village, past the school, the garage – encrusted with wrecked, rusting cars – Mrs Simpson's sell-everything shop, past the crofts and the two churches and turned left to jog on towards Ardtallon.

At last they reached the track that took them over the hills to Miss Tuke's.

'Remember the day we brought them home?' asked Mike. 'They kept on stopping dead and we had to shout, "Trek forward" to make them move.'

'I expect they'll be as bad when we get them back in the autumn,' said Jinny despondently.

About a mile from Miss Tuke's Bramble's head went up and he began to walk out excitedly. By the time they'd reached the drive that led to the trekking centre he was bouncing along, whiffling to himself and making sudden dives to smell the piles of droppings on the hoof-pocked ground.

'They don't half know where they are,' said Mike. 'I've never felt Punch like this before.'

Miss Tuke was waiting for them. She opened the yard gate and the ponies bustled through.

'They are looking well,' she said. 'You've done them proud. I shall need to find two trekkers who can ride to take them over for next week.'

'They're pleased to be home,' said Jinny while Bramble clomped around her, whinnying to a bunch of ponies standing at a gate leading on to moorland.

'Right,' said Miss Tuke when they had taken off the ponies' saddles. 'Here we go. Be heels and teeth,' she warned, as Mike and Jinny led Punch and Bramble through the gate on to the moor and unbridled them.

'Look out!' she warned, as Bramble plunged away from Jinny.

'But I'd got an apple for him,' exclaimed Jinny,

36

staring in dismay as the mob of Highlands went hightailing off up the hill.

'Too late,' said Miss Tuke. 'That's one of the things I like about native ponies. Independent little blighters,' and she laughed as she shut the gate tightly.

'Your Dad says you'll be wanting them back in September.'

'There is just a chance that I might be riding Shantih to school next term,' said Jinny, admitting it to herself now that she had seen Bramble happily reunited with his mates.

'That red squib you had at the show?' demanded Miss Tuke. 'I shall reserve Bramble for you.'

'Has Dad been here long?' asked Mike.

'Quite a wee while. Seems in a hurry. Not his usual self.'

They thanked Miss Tuke again for lending them the ponies and went to find their father. Seeing his face, Jinny got into the back of the car and thought hard about her saddle.

It was two o'clock before they reached Nell Storr's craft shop. Jinny and Mike helped their father to carry in the crates of pottery.

'Oh, lovely,' cried Nell Storr, bearing down on them from a cloud of chiffon that seemed to be floating around her rather than being worn by her. 'Thought you weren't going to make it. I've to be off in a min with someone who's starting up a weaving centre on one of the islands. Free trip to inspect the goodies. As you can see, your shelves are nearly empty again, so fill them up and I'll take another lot as soon as you like.'

'Bless you,' said Mr Manders. 'You do realise that you are the mainstay of all my family.'

'Nonsense,' said Nell. 'I do it for the money. These matching mugs and plates have been madly popular. I know a bod who's branching out into Europe. Shall I send him samples?'

'They're Ken's,' said Mr Manders. 'Do send them.'

'Wonderful glazes he gets,' said Nell, picking up one of Ken's mugs that they had just unpacked and rubbing her hands over the scarlet glaze as she spoke to Mr Manders about special orders.

'Now, Miss Manders,' she said, turning to Jinny. 'What about you? Have you brought me some more drawings?'

Jinny hadn't. Since Easter Nell had been buying Jinny's drawings and selling them in her shop.

'More of that Arab horse. She's their favourite.'

'Well, maybe one lot more,' said Jinny grudgingly. 'I still need more money for my lungeing rein but now I've got the use of Sue's saddle I might buy a martingale.'

'Live dangerously,' encouraged Nell. 'Bring me more drawings and buy both.'

'I'll see,' said Jinny. At first it had seemed a wonderful idea selling her drawings to Nell, but when it actually came to parting with them Jinny wasn't so sure. Sold to Nell they had gone for ever. 'I'll see,' she said again.

It was half-past two before they reached Inverburgh station.

'Platform six,' Mr Manders shouted, running across the crowded station. Jinny and Mike sped after him, dodging in and out between luggage and trollies, passengers and rooted, old men.

They reached platform six just as the Stopton train came in.

'Too late. Here they come,' said the ticket collector, so they had to wait by the barrier, craning their necks to see if any of the people flooding out of the train looked like Marlene or Bill.

'That's them,' cried Jinny. 'Bet you.'

'It is,' said her father, recognising Bill, and then they could all see that the girl beside Bill dragged her left leg as she walked.

Both children were wearing jeans and black nylon anoraks. They were both pale with thick, white, city complexions and spikey, short, brown hair. The boy was slightly taller than his sister. His lower lip stuck out in a defiant, down-turning pout, and even walking along the platform his thick brows were clamped into a scowl. His sister was looking about her anxiously, her face working and her lips twisting as if she was carrying on a conversation with herself.

Mr Manders waved. 'Bill,' he shouted. 'Bill.'

The boy heard him. He looked up, glowering under

his fringe of greasy hair, and without changing his expression he spoke to his sister. She dumped the large, tartan shopper she was carrying on to the platform and waved with both hands. Then, clutching the bag in her arms again, she began to half run, half limp, towards them.

Marlene reached the ticket barrier and produced two tickets from her shopper.

'I ain't half glad you're here. Didn't know what we'd do if you weren't. Them's two tickets, one for me and one for him.' Marlene pointed out Bill to the ticket collector, then she pushed her way through the ticket barrier, holding her shopper well clear of the turnstile.

'Me Mum would have us bring a bag each. Said it wasn't decent unless. One each, like. Pleased to meet you.' Marlene said, holding her hand out to Mr Manders. 'I'm fair dying for a cup of tea. Parched I am with that train. And I need the toilet. Didn't fancy going on that train.'

Mr Manders shook Marlene's hand. 'I'm Mr Manders,' he said. 'And this is Jinny.'

'Pleased to meet you,' said Marlene again.

Jinny grasped the small bony hand with its gnawed fingernails.

'How do you do,' said Jinny distantly, her voice sounding cold and polite.

Marlene's black eyes beetling up at Jinny were hard

as chips of flint. Her thin lips over her decayed teeth were laughing at Jinny. Jinny tried to make her mouth smile but it stuck in a half grimace and she stared across the busy station trying not to show what she was thinking – that already she didn't know how she was going to stick living with Marlene for a fortnight.

'Glad you could come, Bill,' said Mr Manders and introduced Jinny and Mike. Bill grunted, standing behind his sister, not looking up.

'Eh now,' said Marlene, 'now that we've got the la-di-dahs over how about the toilet and a bite of food?'

She grinned round, her eyes plucking at each person's face until she made them respond to her.

'Then it's me for the rodeo, ain't it? I'm proper churned up about it. Me on that fancy horse,' and Marlene clutched up her tartan shopper and slapping her hand on her thigh she limped off to the Ladies.

'Better go with her,' said Mr Manders.

Cold with embarrassment, Jinny turned to follow Marlene, trying not to see the people who were staring as she gave Wild West whoops and hirpled her way through the crowds.

# *Three*

'Have you seen Marlene?' Mrs Manders asked Jinny when she came down for breakfast the next morning. 'We thought she must be with you.'

'Well, she's not,' said Jinny, glancing quickly round the table and realising that there were only two empty places – her own and Marlene's.

'We thought you might have been out with Shantih,' went on Jinny's mother.

'You were wrong. I haven't seen her.'

Yesterday, when they had got back to Finmory, Marlene had demanded a ride on Shantih.

'I'm not taking her out again today,' Jinny had stated. 'I was riding her this morning. She's not a bicycle, you know.'

'Never thought he was,' Marlene had replied. 'Ain't never seen a bicycle that looked like that. Don't see why I can't have a ride now. He's walking round the field, ain't he? Why can't I sit on him?'

'Because,' said Jinny finally and took herself off to her bedroom to clean her saddle.

'Bill, have you seen your sister?' persisted Mrs Manders.

'Naw,' said Bill, a slice of thickly-buttered toast in one hand a forkload of tomatoes and bacon in the other.

'Jinny, go and see if she's in her room.'

'Why can't Petra?' complained Jinny automatically but without hope.

'Marlene,' Jinny called as she ran upstairs. 'Marlene.' But there was no reply. Jinny knocked on her bedroom door, then opened it. Marlene's bed was neatly made, her tartan shopper sitting on top of the quilt. Propped up on the dressing table was a blurry photograph of Marlene, Bill, a thin woman with a wintry face and a large, bleary man. Jinny looked at it intently, then, remembering what she was meant to be doing, went back down to tell her family that Marlene wasn't there.

'Try the garden,' said her mother.

'I haven't had my breakfast and Sue's coming up.'

'It won't take you a second,' said Mrs Manders.

'Jinny,' said her father, and Jinny went.

*Some holiday this is going to be*, she thought rebelliously. *I'll bet she's with Shantih. I'll bet they make me give her a ride and when she falls off and hurts herself it will be Shantih's fault.*

There was no sign of Marlene in the garden and Jinny went on past the stables, down to the ponies' field.

Marlene was sitting on top of the field gate. In the middle of the field Shantih was standing, watching her warily. Marlene looked quickly over her shoulder at the sound of Jinny's approach, then dropped down into the field. She landed on her hands and knees, scrambled up and began to run towards the Arab.

'Look out,' yelled Jinny. 'She'll kick you. Don't run at her like that.'

Marlene paused to scowl at Jinny then went on limping across the field towards the horse.

Shantih's front feet were planted close together, her neck stretched out, her pointed ears nearly touching. Jinny knew that when she stood like that, she could swing round and whirl away in a split second, hooves flying as she galloped off.

'Be careful,' shouted Jinny, but Marlene paid no attention to her. She was holding out a sugar lump to Shantih. Half limping, half running she blundered towards the Arab.

'Stop running,' Jinny shouted. 'Walk!'

But Marlene went on stumbling and tripping in her haste to reach Shantih.

'Have a sugar lump,' Marlene was saying. 'Sweeten you up so it will.'

As Jinny reached the field she paused uncertainly, knowing how Shantih's hooves could flash out quicker than lightning when she was frightened, and not wanting to risk chasing Marlene.

'Oh, slow down,' she cried.

'Shut up. I'm giving him a sugar lump, ain't I,' Marlene yelled back.

'Her,' said Jinny, and to her horror she saw Marlene's lame foot catch in a tussock of grass, saw her go falling, sprawling towards Shantih, her arms outstretched, catching at the Arab's shoulder and legs as she fell.

The shoes on Shantih's hind feet glinted in the sun as she lashed out, missing Marlene's head by inches as she lay in the grass.

Jinny vaulted over the gate, ran at Shantih, shouting, chasing her away, but already the mare had thundered off to the far corner of the field, where she waited, quarters turned against the girls, the whites of her eyes rolling wildly.

'Are you all right?' demanded Jinny, helping Marlene to her feet. 'I told you to stop running at her. That was enough to frighten any horse.'

Marlene shook herself free.

'Get off me,' she muttered. 'I only fell, didn't I? Where's me sugar? I'm going to give it to the horse.'

Jinny picked up the sugar lump. 'You've to come in for breakfast,' she said.

'Give us me sugar,' said Marlene. 'I'll just pop it in first,' and she set off again towards Shantih.

Jinny grabbed hold of her arms. 'You were nearly

kicked,' she exclaimed. 'Don't you realise that if Shantih had got you she could have killed you? You can't treat a horse like that.'

'Give over,' said Marlene, 'pulling at me.'

'You've got to come in to breakfast *now*,' said Jinny, keeping her hold on Marlene's arm.

'What about the old horse? Got to get his sugar lump, ain't he?'

'She doesn't care whether she has a sugar lump or not. She doesn't want your sugar.'

Marlene's black eyes bulleted into Jinny.

'Let me go,' she demanded. 'I got to give the horse his sugar. Like it says in the papers – "Be kind to a little donkey" – well, I'm being kind to a little horse if you'll only let off holding me.'

'But she doesn't . . .' words failed Jinny. She let go of Marlene. 'Well, wait there till I get a halter,' she said.

'Halter?' said Marlene.

'Rope,' said Jinny, 'to hold her with while you give her your precious sugar lump. Now promise, stand there till I get back. Promise?'

'Get a move on then,' grinned Marlene.

Jinny caught Shantih with a handful of oats and led her towards Marlene.

'Hold your hand out flat,' said Jinny irritably. 'And put the sugar lump on it.'

'Bit dirty that,' said Marlene, holding out the sugar lump between finger and thumb.

'No,' said Jinny. 'Not that way.'

Shantih made a grab at the sugar. Marlene dropped it and Shantih snuffled it up and crunched it.

'Now,' said Jinny. 'Let's go and have our breakfast while you are still in one piece. She nearly took your fingers off that time. Not that you'd notice.'

Jinny took Shantih's halter off and the horse walked beside them to the gate.

'See, I was right,' said Marlene. 'He right enjoyed that sugar. He's after more.'

Mrs Manders suggested that Marlene should wash her hands before she started on her cornflakes.

'They don't need it,' said Marlene sitting down. 'I held the sugar lump out ever so dainty. Old horse didn't muck me up at all. If I'd done it the way she told me I'd have been in a right mess then.'

Jinny, sitting slumped in her chair, groaned to herself. Already Marlene had nearly been kicked to death and almost had her fingers bitten off. *And whose fault would it be?* thought Jinny. *It would all be Shantih's fault.*

'And what are you doing this morning?' Mrs Manders asked.

'Mike and I are going for a walk up the hill,' said Mr Manders to Bill. 'Some wood to chop first. How about helping and then coming up the hill?'

'Naw,' said Bill.

'Not after being in hospital he ain't. Doctor wouldn't

have it,' Marlene explained. 'He can come and watch me riding. Be some fireworks when I get up on the old horse, I bet.'

'Will you stop calling Shantih an old horse,' cried Jinny.

'Didn't mean no offence,' said Marlene. 'Bit touchy, ain't she?' Marlene winked at Ken.

Jinny took a deep breath and another slice of toast.

'I'm just telling you,' she said. 'Just so that you'll all know, that I don't think Marlene is fit to ride Shantih. I think she'll get hurt. And it won't be my fault when it happens.'

'Don't listen to her,' said Petra. 'She's got this thing about Shantih. Has to keep her all to herself.'

'I've told you,' repeated Jinny. 'It will not be my fault when she hurts herself.'

'I'll come and help,' offered Petra, smiling at Marlene. 'I'll hold you on. You'll be quite safe.'

'That,' said Jinny, 'is all I need. Two of you who know nothing about horses.'

When Jinny had groomed Shantih and put her tack on she led her down to the field with Petra and Marlene walking beside her. Mike, Ken and Bill were waiting at the gate.

'I'll ride her round first,' said Jinny, mounting, and easing her fingers on the reins she let Shantih walk forward. The Arab was uneasy about the group watching from the gate and still troubled by the strange

48

disappearance of Punch and Bramble.

'There's the horse,' murmured Jinny. 'Gently the good horse.'

Shantih mouthed at the snaffle and Jinny let her trot on. They crossed the field and trotted round in the other direction. Riding Shantih, Jinny was aware of nothing but the rhythm of her horse; the brightness and freedom of riding her.

Jinny sat down and asked Shantih to canter. She was ready when the mare plunged and shied. Sitting deep in her new saddle, Jinny gathered her together between seat and fingers and sent her on, flowing round the field at a steady canter.

As they passed the gate Petra shouted that it was Marlene's turn, distracting Jinny, and at the same moment Kelly emerged from the hedge. Shantih reared. Jinny, secure in her saddle, hardly moved. Shantih reared again, without much enthusiasm, and Jinny sent her on to canter for a last time round the field.

While Shantih had been rearing, Jinny had caught a glimpse of Marlene's face. It had been clenched tight with fear.

*Why does she want to ride when she's afraid?* thought Jinny. *And with her leg!*

'Are you sure you do want to ride?' Jinny demanded when she got back to Marlene. 'You don't have to, you know.'

But already Marlene was limping towards her.

'Thought you weren't never going to give me a shot,' she said as Jinny dismounted. 'Poor old thing'll be worn out by the time it's me turn.'

Petra had brought a length of rope from the stables and was knotting it efficiently through Shantih's bit ring.

'Better put the stirrups down,' she told Jinny. 'Now, reins in your left hand and face her tail,' she instructed Marlene.

Marlene grabbed a bundle of reins with a shaking hand.

'Left foot into the stirrup,' bossed Petra, 'and spring up into the saddle.'

'She can't . . .' began Jinny, who was holding Shantih's head.

'Me wonky leg,' said Marlene. 'No use this side,' and she ducked down under Shantih's neck and before Jinny had realised what was happening she had pulled herself up on the off side and was sitting astride Shantih.

'Eh, he ain't half high,' squeaked Marlene. 'When we going to get moving, eh? Gee up, old horse.'

'Don't hit her,' cried Jinny desperately as Marlene flapped Shantih's reins on her neck, but her warning was too late. Shantih, terrified by anything that reminded her of the circus master's whip, had flung away from Jinny in bunching, twisting fear.

'Hold the saddle,' Jinny yelled and grabbed at the rope to help Petra to control Shantih.

'Whoa. Steady, steady,' Jinny soothed as she caught at Shantih's bridle. 'Steady now. It's all right.'

At last Shantih stood still. She was tense and shivering, her nostrils wide, her eyes bulging from her head and, somehow, Marlene was still on top.

'What did you have to go and do that for?' Jinny demanded. Her hands gentled Shantih as she glared furiously at Marlene's white face. 'Giving her a fright like that.'

Mike had come dashing across to help. Only Ken still leaned on the gate, his face calm, his eyes unconnected to the turmoil in the field.

'How was I to know I shouldn't hit him? You want to see them on the telly. They wallop them good. Thought I was doing it right.'

'Well, you weren't,' snapped Jinny.

'I think you were wonderful staying on like that,' praised Petra. 'Wonderful. I'd have been off.'

Marlene beamed. 'Perhaps it's going to be me thing, this horse-riding. Got to get him moving though, ain't we?' And for a horrible moment Jinny thought she was going to slap the reins down again on Shantih's neck.

'Don't,' cried Jinny.

But suddenly Marlene seemed to have lost interest in Shantih.

'Where's our Bill?' Marlene demanded, straining forward. 'He ain't there.'

They all looked at the gate and realised that she was right. Bill wasn't there, only Ken.

'Gone off somewhere on his own, I suppose,' said Mike.

Marlene slithered to the ground and limped to the gate.

'Our Bill,' she said. 'Where's he off to?'

'Why?' said Ken.

'You know,' said Marlene.

Ken eased himself off the gate. 'I'll find him,' he said.

'Proper decent of you,' said Marlene. 'It's OK,' she said to Mike, 'Ken'll keep an eye on him.' And she ran back to Shantih.

There was the sound of trotting hooves, Pippen's squealing whinny, and Sue rode up.

'Morning,' she said, smiling round.

'Come on,' said Marlene. 'Let's get on with me riding. We've been mucking round here long enough.'

'Honestly!' exclaimed Jinny in disgust, wanting to introduce Sue to her family, not wanting any more to do with Marlene's riding. 'Can't you wait a minute? Perhaps Sue will let you have a ride on Pippen. He'd be much more suitable.'

'Ride that fat old thing?' said Marlene. 'I wouldn't have it at me funeral.' And she hoisted herself determinedly back on to Shantih. 'Gee up, then,' she said. 'Gee up.'

# Four

Pippen snorted, digging his toes into the peaty hillside, bumbling along as he tried to keep up with Shantih's long stride.

'Look!' exclaimed Sue, turning to gaze back the way they had ridden. Rolling moorland fell away beneath them, hummocked with sheep and jagged with rocks. Finmory House and Mr MacKenzie's farm were toy buildings standing in patchwork fields. The sea crinkled between the black jaws of Finmory Bay, then stretched out, a shimmering, flickering blue, to the far horizon.

'Uh-huh,' agreed Jinny. Normally a day like this made her frothy with delight at living surrounded by such wide freedom; at riding Shantih over the moors; at having escaped from the dirt and traffic of Stopton, but today she hardly noticed it. She had Marlene on her mind.

'There's our tent,' pointed Sue.

Jinny supposed it was. Marlene had had two more rides on Shantih and was becoming bored with being led round the field. 'We've been stuck in this old field for two days,' she had said to Jinny earlier that morning. 'Might as well be on a roundabout. When we going to go a proper ride?' she kept demanding.

'Can't you see I'm having a job keeping her quiet enough for you when we're in the field? If I took you on to the beach and she started playing up there I couldn't hold on to her, what would happen then?'

'How about Petra? She could hang on too.'

'You seem to think that everyone should spend all their time running after you. How about Bill helping for a change?'

'Not with his lungs,' warned Marlene. 'Doctor wouldn't have it.'

Jinny had not been surprised to hear that. It seemed to Jinny that the only thing that Bill was allowed to do was to sit around reading his pile of American comics under Marlene's protective eye.

'And,' Jinny told Sue, 'she won't leave Shantih alone. Keeps on wanting to give her sugar.'

'Marlene?' asked Sue. 'She's OK, I like her.'

'You don't know her,' retorted Jinny indignantly. 'It's not your horse that she's messing about with. When she falls off and breaks her back they'll say it was because Shantih is wild and uncontrollable, and it won't be that at all. It will be all Marlene's fault.'

Sue laughed at Jinny's expression of gloom. 'Shantih hasn't bucked once today,' she said, hoping to cheer Jinny up.

'Pollyanna,' said Jinny scornfully and she glowered over the bright sunlit moor, seeing nothing but Marlene annoying her horse.

'We can canter here,' Jinny called back when they reached a flat stretch of moor, and she let Shantih plunge forward into a gallop.

Pippen's hooves drumming behind her filled Shantih with a sudden excitement. She stretched her neck and raced forward. Jinny felt her hair banner out behind her with their speed, the whole moorland blurred as Shantih scorched over it. Jinny crouched forward, her knees secure against the knee rolls, her knuckles digging into her horse's shoulders. Normally when Shantih took off like this Jinny was completely out of control, being carted wherever Shantih cared to take her, but now, with Sue's saddle, Jinny had the purchase to collect her horse and feel her respond to the bit's pressure even at a flat-out gallop.

They reached the end of the canter, where normally Jinny had to fight Shantih, turning her uphill into the boggy hillside to steady her up. But today Jinny sat down deep into the saddle and was able to use her reins and seat to bring Shantih back to a trot. Within a few strides they were walking again.

Exultant, Jinny turned to see Pippen rocking sedately along at a collected canter.

'Did you see that!' Jinny cried.

'She's like a racehorse,' exclaimed Sue, catching up.

'Oh, not that,' said Jinny. 'She can go faster than that. I mean the way we stopped. And it's all your saddle.'

With Sue telling tales of her Pony Club at home, they rode towards the standing stones.

'Wish there was a Pony Club here,' said Jinny.

'Don't be daft. We just make up things to do,' said Sue, 'because we don't have anywhere real to ride. I'd swop all Mrs Moss's instruction for even the littlest bit of this moor.'

And Jinny knew that what Sue said was true.

They dismounted at the standing stones and, holding their horses' reins, sat down in the sun to share a bar of chocolate.

Jinny shuddered as she looked at the sun-glossed moorland and the floating, mauve-shadowed mountains, remembering how it had been in the winter – a terrifying desert of snow.

'What's up?' asked Sue.

'Some day,' said Jinny quickly, to drive the snow ghosts away, 'I'm going to ride up here and camp.' She imagined herself curled up, warm and safe, in her sleeping-bag while Shantih grazed close by.

'Oh yes!' agreed Sue.

'That is,' said Jinny, 'when I can find a tent. If I ever can find a tent.'

'But I've got one.'

'You're all sleeping in it. You can't expect your mother and father to sleep in the car while we take their tent!'

'Not that one, stupid. We've got a small one. Plenty of room in it for us.'

'Could we?' said Jinny. 'Now, while the weather's good?'

'Why not?'

'Yes, let's. Let's.'

'Tomorrow,' suggested Sue.

'We wouldn't need much,' said Jinny.

'A kettle and a pan,' said Sue. 'We could have a campfire and cook our food on it. Pippen can be a pack pony.'

The two girls grinned at each other.

'If we camp here we can ride further into the hills,' said Jinny. 'Further than I've ever ridden before.'

'Pippen's been to Pony Club camp,' said Sue. 'He's used to being tethered.'

Jinny wasn't so sure about Shantih, but she pushed the doubt hurriedly to the back of her mind.

'We can camp for as long as we like,' said Sue. 'We'll send up smoke signals to let them know we're surviving.'

'Go wooding,' said Jinny. 'There's plenty of dead branches from the pines round Loch Varrich.'

Then suddenly Jinny thought about Marlene. Marlene would want to come with them. Jinny got up to make sure that Shantih's girth wasn't too tight, which she knew it wasn't because she had just loosened it a minute ago. Whatever happened Jinny didn't want Marlene spoiling their camp. She fiddled with the girth buckles, trying not to think how Marlene would stand watching them ride off to camp in the hills.

*I don't care*, Jinny thought. *She's not coming with us*. And she sat down again beside Sue.

'What about Marlene?' asked Sue, knowing Jinny's thoughts.

'Oh, she wouldn't want to come,' cried Jinny, defending herself. 'She couldn't possibly come all this way when she's got that bad leg. And I don't suppose she'd want to sleep in a tent.'

Sue twisted the buckle on Pippen's reins, not looking at Jinny.

'I'm sure she wouldn't want to come,' insisted Jinny. 'She can't come, anyway, and that's that.'

Sue didn't answer and for a moment there was only the sound of their horses cropping the short moorland turf, the high, twittering lark song, and, far off, a curlew's liquid, bubbling notes.

Jinny jumped to her feet.

'Come on,' she said. 'If we're camping tomorrow we'll need to get a move on. I think Mum's going to the shop this afternoon so she could buy some tins for us.'

'Couldn't we each put a pound into the kitty and buy our own food?' Sue asked as they remounted. 'I can afford it because I've got my holiday money.'

Jinny thought of saying that she couldn't afford a pound and that she'd bring some food from home, but it sounded so much more independent going to Mrs Simpson's to buy their own food. She would need to open the tin box where she kept the money she was saving towards a lungeing rein for Shantih.

'And I've some money from the drawings I sold to the craft shop,' she admitted.

'We'll need to make a list of things,' said Sue as they rode home.

'Bread, dried milk and butter,' said Jinny.

'A raspberry jelly,' suggested Sue. 'To eat not make.'

'Dried apple rings. They swell up inside you in case we're starving.'

'And marzipan,' said Sue.

Sue's parents were quite agreeable for her to camp at the standing stones but felt that it would be rather nice if she spent the rest of the day with them, so Sue gave Jinny her money, telling her to be sure to buy marzipan if she could possibly manage it.

When Jinny got back home she tipped some oats for Shantih onto the grass and left her eating them. She hung her bridle on its hook and carried the saddle up to her bedroom.

'Had a good ride?' asked her mother, who was

vacuuming the landing. Jinny said she had and went on up to her room. She stood on a chair to reach the top of her wardrobe and lifted down her cash box. Originally it had belonged to Petra, but when the lock had broken she had abandoned it to Jinny who swathed it in sellotape to stop herself getting into it.

Hesitating, Jinny thought of asking her father to give her the money, then she jumped down off the chair and ripped off the sellotape in a scrumpled, sticky mess.

'You are getting too mean to live,' she told herself. 'You'll be hiring out Shantih next.' And she opened the box and took out a pound.

The sellotape was too messed up to be used again. Jinny considered putting the box back as it was, but she knew that if she did the money left in it would soon be spent.

*Need to find some more*, she thought. *Better stick it up again.* And she remembered seeing a roll of sellotape in the pottery room.

Ken was working at the wheel.

'Hi,' he said, looking up at Jinny and smiling his slow smile that seemed to light up his green eyes and spread easily over his whole face. He set you before him, making space for you to be yourself. Not the quick, half-afraid twitch that most people made at you. 'Bit of a stranger,' he suggested.

''Spose so,' agreed Jinny, looking round for the

sellotape, 'and you'll be seeing less of me. We're going to camp at the standing stones.'

'We?'

'Might camp for nights and nights if the weather stays fine.'

Jinny's eyes flicked over the batches of pots waiting to be fired, over the glowing rows of glazed pottery and the plastic bins of clay. She searched the mess of the windowsill with its frosting of powdered clay, jars of glaze and bits of broken pots. The table, too, was littered. Jinny moved things about, searching.

'Have you seen that roll of sellotape?' she asked.

'We?' said Ken again.

'You're bound to find out,' said Jinny in exasperation. 'We means Sue and myself and not Marlene. She couldn't come all that way. Not with her leg.'

'You have to camp as far away as the standing stones?' said Ken, treadling the wheel, doodling the clay between his long, gentle fingers, but Jinny could feel his eyes on her.

'Yes,' she said. 'We have to camp at the standing stones. We've arranged it.' And to her relief she spotted the sellotape.

'Feel free,' said Ken. 'Do what you like.'

'Will do,' said Jinny, already halfway out of the door.

Jinny told them at lunchtime that she was going camping. Eating stew and potatoes gave her hands something to do while she was telling them.

'What about water?' asked Mr Manders, and Jinny's mother wondered about warmth and having enough to eat.

'I'm coming with you to Mrs Simpson's this afternoon,' said Jinny. 'I've got a list of supplies and we're only camping while it's fine, so we will be quite all right.'

'What'll we take for the old horse?' asked Marlene. 'Won't be much grass up on them mountains for him. I'd better take him plenty of sugar lumps.'

For one moment Jinny hadn't been able to stop herself looking up at Marlene. Just long enough to see her face brighten with expectation at the thought of going with Shantih over the moors.

'Oh, we'll take oats for the horses,' Jinny said, staring down at her plate. She was being polite and brisk. Not using her own voice. For that was the way you dealt with situations like this. You were polite but firm, and then everyone knew where they stood. 'I'm going with Sue. We'll only be away for a night or two. It's too far for you, I'm afraid.'

'Oh, Jinny!' cried Mrs Manders in dismay. 'Of course Marlene can go with you. Of course you can, dear.'

Jinny forced herself not to look up.

'Don't "Oh Jinny" her for me,' shrilled Marlene. 'I wouldn't want to go trailing up them mountains, not for nothing. I just pity that poor old horse, that's all.'

'There you are,' said Jinny. 'I knew she wouldn't want to come.' But she kept her eyes clamped tight on to her hands, gripping her knife and fork until her knuckles shone through her skin and her nails bit into her palms.

Mrs Manders cornered Jinny as she finished the washing up.

'I am thoroughly ashamed of you,' she said. 'Really I am. How could you be so cruel?'

'I'm being kind,' said Jinny. 'If she goes on making me give her rides on Shantih she's going to fall off and hurt herself. So I'm being kind to her, taking Shantih away so that she can't ride her.'

Mrs Manders turned her back and walked away. Every bit of Jinny ached to run after her and try to explain how it really was true; that Marlene really would be hurt if she went on riding Shantih; that it was dangerous; that Shantih wasn't a pony like Miss Tuke's trekkers who would plod along with beginners on their backs not caring what their riders did. Shantih was a highly-strung Arab horse. You couldn't mess about with her. She could so easily be frightened and then it would be too late, Marlene would be injured.

But Jinny couldn't make herself move. She stood fiddling with her hair.

'When are you going to Mrs Simpson's?' she called after her mother, her voice flat as if she was speaking to a stranger.

'About three,' replied Mrs Manders without stopping.

Mr and Mrs Manders, Jinny and Marlene, taking an unwilling Bill with her, all packed into the car.

'After we've done the shopping we'll drive on for a bit. Let you see the country round about,' said Mrs Manders to Bill. 'We'll go round by the Crawlin rocks. Fantastic scenery there. Black gaping caves. You can stand on the cliffs and hear the sea booming under your feet.'

Bill didn't bother to reply. Since he had arrived Jinny had hardly heard him speak at all. The only time he showed any enthusiasm was when Mrs Manders called him for his meals and whenever he had stuffed the last bite in his mouth he went back to reading his comics and scratching his head.

'Anything special you'd like to do, Bill?' Mr Manders asked. 'We're open to suggestions. There's a wildlife park about thirty miles away. We could go there for the day? Or a sail?'

'Doctor wouldn't have that,' said Marlene. 'He's OK, ain't you, Bill? He's better taking it easy like. Doctor said he wasn't to strain himself. Couldn't go pulling up anchors and all that.'

'Not a yacht,' Mr Manders assured her. 'A sail on a steamer. Bill could sit in an armchair as we sailed along.'

'Naw,' said Bill.

'Better not,' said Marlene.

'Perhaps Mrs Simpson will have some comics you haven't read,' suggested Mrs Manders.

'He likes the ones he's got, thank you all the same,' said Marlene.

Mr Manders trod on the accelerator and wondered what they were doing wrong. He knew what Jinny was doing wrong – smuggling Shantih off to the hills so that she didn't have to share her with Marlene. Part of him was furious with his daughter for being so selfish, part was standing back waiting to see what would happen next and part of him wasn't even surprised.

To possess a loved one; to possess completely and absolutely, so that you didn't care what you did as long as you could say MINE, seemed to be deep at the centre of every human being. Except the few. The very few.

'Tom!' shouted his wife. 'Look where you're going. We were right off the road then.'

And Mr Manders remembered he was driving.

'Come away in with you now,' Mrs Simpson said, as they all crowded into her shop.

Mrs Simpson's was the only shop in Glenbost and it sold everything. Slippers and paraffin heaters, cheese and liqueur chocolates, pork chops and cabbages, men's long winter drawers and women's Sunday hats, stamps and pensions were all to be had at Mrs Simpson's. Some of her stock had taken up more or less permanent residence, some had lodgers. Petra had found a dead mouse in a net of oranges.

'Wasn't that the lucky thing now that the wee fellow died in the oranges,' Mrs Simpson had said when Petra pointed it out to her. 'And them done up so tidy in their skins. I'd have been worried myself if he'd been living in with the sausages.'

Mrs Simpson leaned over her counter and examined Bill and Marlene with a hard stare. She had almost accepted the Manders as harmless lunatics but she was still suspicious of any of their visitors. She feared that the families she referred to as heathen hippies, who had lived at Finmory before the Manders, were still lurking in the hills ready to make a comeback.

'It's the beautiful day,' she admitted grudgingly. 'But I'm thinking myself it won't last much longer.'

'See you've been branching out into a new line,' said Mr Manders.

'Indeed I have. Not new because we were having them before, but perhaps you wouldn't be here then.'

Jinny couldn't think how her father could possibly notice whether Mrs Simpson had anything new or not since all her stock was scrabbled and jumbled together. Then she saw what he meant. On the counter was a smart perspex case with about a dozen watches in it. On top of the case, displayed in its own box, was a man's gold watch. Mr Manders picked it up.

'Very nice,' he said.

'Now there's the coincidence,' said Mrs Simpson. 'When the salesman showed me that very one, it was yourself I saw walk into this shop, Mr Manders, put it on, and walk out a man with the pride about him.'

'Joke taken,' said Mr Manders. 'How much?'

'To you, eighty-two pounds. It has the wee bookie with it to tell you the value of it. Jewels like Aladdin's cave and the everlasting calendar so that you need never be wasting your money on the paper rubbish ever again.'

'Yes. Well,' said Mr Manders putting the watch back in its box. 'How much do I owe you for looking at it?'

'Eh, give us a see,' said Bill, snatching the watch from Mr Manders. 'That's what I call a watch, that is. I'll have one of them. You'll see.'

Mrs Simpson swiftly removed the watch from Bill, put it back in its box and replaced it reverently on top of the case.

'How much did you say?' demanded Bill.

'Who will ever buy that here?' exclaimed Mrs Manders. 'It's a beautiful watch,' she added quickly, in case Mrs Simpson should take umbrage and plunge the Manders into sudden famine. 'But eighty-two pounds!'

'Goodness yes,' stated Mrs Simpson coldly. 'It's five hundred pounds they're paying for them in the cities.'

'It's a tourist trap,' guessed Mr Manders.

'You could be saying that, but if there's not a tourist in my trap by October I'm thinking eighty-two pounds is about the exact sum the congregation will be giving to the Reverend James when he comes to the retirement in November. And him, poor man, without a watch to his name.'

Mr Manders burst out laughing.

'Laugh you may,' said Mrs Simpson, not even smiling, 'but that's the good business sense.' And she took the watch away again from Bill. 'Leave it be,' she said sharply. 'Keep your fingers to yourself in my shop.'

Quickly, Mrs Manders began to read out her order.

When her mother had finished Jinny fished out her list.

'I want some things too,' she said, and began with the bread-and-butter essentials.

On the wall behind Mrs Simpson was a mirror hung round with pairs of wellington boots on a string so that there was only a small space left to reflect the front of the shop, but enough for a movement in it to catch Jinny's attention. In the mirror she saw Bill reaching up for the watch again, saw Marlene catch hold of his hand and snatch it away from the case. There was a tightness at the corners of Marlene's lips, a pinched, indrawn shadow at her cheeks and nostrils, her black bead eyes were narrowed and her brows knotted down. Jinny hadn't seen her looking like that before but she had seen that look somewhere, that cold, defeated, bitterness.

'You'll be setting up your own establishment with

all this food?' said Mrs Simpson, waiting to be told why Jinny was buying it.

'We're going camping on the moors,' said Jinny.

'With that terrible wild horse?'

'And a friend,' said Jinny.

From the mirror, Marlene's indrawn mask stared straight at her and suddenly Jinny knew where she had seen that look before. It had been on the woman's face in the photograph on Marlene's dressing table.

# Five

Just after ten the next morning, Sue led Pippen towards Finmory and Jinny, watching from the stable doorway, thought that he looked like the original clothes horse or the White Knight's horse from *Alice*.

'Even the kitchen sink,' Sue yelled, waving a plastic bucket. 'Did you get the supplies?'

'Couldn't afford marzipan,' Jinny told her. 'Anyway, the lump Mrs Simpson had looked mousley. She'd had it since Christmas. But I got two jellies. A lemon and a raspberry.'

'Same to you,' giggled Sue. 'Are you nearly ready?'

'I've brought Shantih in,' Jinny said, 'and I've packed all the things in a rucksack. I think she'll let me tie my sleeping bag on to the front of the saddle but not much else. Just need to hang them on myself seeing Pippen is fully occupied.'

'Isn't he?' said Sue lovingly. 'Took me ages to pack him. It's times like this, when he's so totally obliging, that I try to remember when we're last in races. Mummy says they will be coming up the mountain to borrow back their stuff.'

'You've even brought a kettle,' said Jinny, examining Pippen's load more closely.

'Do not look down the spout. It has white furry knickers all over it.'

'Yuch,' said Jinny. 'Thanks for the warning.'

She put Shantih's tack on, then, very cautiously tied her sleeping bag to the front of the saddle. Shantih rolled her eyes back suspiciously, but apart from this didn't object.

'She was OK,' Jinny announced to Sue, who didn't seem to care. *I expect it's being used to Pippen,* Jinny thought. *If she'd known Shantih last autumn she'd realise what it means being able to put a saddle on her, never mind a sleeping bag.*

'I'm going for my hat,' Jinny said to Sue. 'And then I think we're ready.'

'I haven't got a pan,' said Sue. 'Could you bring one?'

'Frying?'

'That's all we'll need, isn't it? Be mostly sandwiches.'

'Cordon bleu,' said Jinny, 'but between bread.' And she ran up to the house.

'A frying pan,' said her mother, finding an old one.

'Matches?' asked her father, and Jinny said she

thought Sue would have some because she seemed to have most things, but in case Sue hadn't any she'd take some.

'Come straight home if the weather changes,' warned Mrs Manders.

Jinny said they would. Then there was a pause when her family should have been telling her to enjoy herself, planning to join them for a campfire sing-song or giving her a surprise food parcel to be opened at camp. Jinny would even have welcomed one of Petra's comments, but she could hear the piano and knew that Petra must be practising. Jinny hadn't seen Ken that morning. In a way she didn't mind. She didn't particularly want to see him.

'Well,' Jinny said, sitting her hard hat in the frying pan and holding it as if she was entering for an egg and spoon race. 'I'd better fry.'

Nobody even smiled.

'Bye,' said Jinny, not really looking at her parents, more taking them in as she glanced round the kitchen before escaping back to Sue.

Marlene and Bill were standing at the stables.

*Oh no!* thought Jinny. As if they hadn't caused enough trouble already. Why couldn't Marlene leave the horses alone? Jinny stomped down the path pulling her hard hat down over her eyes.

'This you off, then?' asked Marlene. 'Going to give us a last shot before you go?' Her black eyes clawed at Jinny's face forcing her to answer. 'Better have a ride now, eh? Old thing'll be worn out when he comes back from them mountains. Won't be fit for me to ride, he won't.'

'She,' retorted Jinny furiously. Her temper surged up, making her want to run at Marlene and shake her by the shoulders, yelling that she couldn't ride Shantih because Shantih was hers and Marlene was to leave her alone.

'Round the field, like?' said Marlene. 'Go on, just once before you go off?'

'No!' shouted Jinny. 'No! No! No!'

'Look,' suggested Sue hurriedly, 'I'll take Pippen's saddle off and you can have a ride bareback.'

'Naw,' said Marlene. 'He's all hairy and he's too fat. I'd be split up me middle sitting on him.'

'You see,' said Jinny smugly. 'It's no use trying to be nice to her.'

But Sue didn't seem to mind. She was laughing at Marlene.

'Perhaps you're right,' she said to Marlene, and then to Jinny, 'Give her a ride round the field. It won't take a minute. I don't mind waiting.'

'Well!' said Jinny. 'Well honestly.' And she banged down the frying pan, making Pippen jump.

Muttering to herself, Jinny led Shantih down the path to the field.

'Bill,' shouted Marlene. 'Come and watch me. I'm

for the riding again.' And Bill followed them down to the field, still reading his comic.

*This is bad enough*, thought Jinny, *but it would be much worse if he wanted to ride too*. And she imagined Bill sitting slumped on Shantih, scratching his head and reading his comic.

'Here we are, old horse,' said Marlene. 'Up and over.'

Despite her lame leg, Marlene could mount from the off side without any difficulty. She swung her leg over Shantih's back, taking care not to touch the horse's quarters with her foot, found her stirrup without looking down and gathered up her reins, holding them correctly.

'Walk on,' Jinny said to Shantih and led the Arab forward by the halter rope she was wearing underneath her bridle.

'Wait on me there, Bill,' Marlene called, casting one last, quick look at her brother before she gave all her attention to Shantih.

Jinny walked at Shantih's side paying no attention to Marlene.

'How about some speed?' asked Marlene.

Jinny clenched her teeth and pretended not to hear. She thought hard about camping with Sue, of sleeping in the tent and riding out tomorrow to discover what lay beyond Loch Varrich. Mr MacKenzie had told her that before the clearances there had been a village in the hills. Perhaps they would discover the ruined crofts.

Jinny stepped over the moss-covered stones that had once been the walls of the crofts. Her eye caught the glint of silver and she pounced on a brooch that had fallen from a woman's shawl when she was being driven out to the ship that had waited in Finmory Bay to take the crofters to America.

Jinny had completely blocked out Marlene.

Suddenly the halter rope scorched through her hand as Shantih leaped forward at a ragged trot. Just in time, Jinny managed to hold on to the tail end of the rope and to dash forward beside her. For a second Jinny thought that Shantih had bounded forward by herself, and then she saw Marlene's face. She was grinning with delight, her bullet eyes sparkling, her mouth laughing.

'Gee up,' Marlene shouted out as she bounced enthusiastically up and down in the saddle.

*Right*, thought Jinny. *I'll show her. I'll teach her a lesson*. And instead of trying to slow Shantih back to a walk she went on running at her side, keeping her trotting, urging the Arab to go faster.

'Eh, watch out, I'll be off,' gasped Marlene.

*Good*, thought Jinny. *Serve you right*.

Marlene grabbed at the pommel of the saddle. Her shrill sounds of alarm coming out in sudden jerks as she bumped about.

Back at the gate Jinny checked Shantih to a sudden halt.

'That's it,' she said. 'Get down.'

Marlene slithered to the ground.

'Did you mean to trot?' Sue asked. 'Marlene nearly fell. She'd no idea how to post.'

'She wanted to go fast so I let her,' said Jinny.

'Oh,' said Sue.

Jinny ran up Shantih's stirrups, took her reins over her head and swung the loaded rucksack onto her own back. She knew what Sue was thinking but she didn't care. Jinny hoped that she'd given Marlene a fright. She hoped it would stop Marlene wanting to ride Shantih. Or, better still, make her want to go back to Stopton so that Jinny never needed to see her again.

'Gracious,' exclaimed Mrs Manders. 'Are you two still here?' She looked from her scowling daughter to Marlene, who had collapsed flat on the grass.

'Jin was giving Marlene a last ride,' explained Sue. 'We're going now.'

'We hope,' said Jinny. 'That is if we can get away.'

'Marlene and Bill,' said Mrs Manders, paying no attention to Jinny's grumbling. 'We're going down to the shop. Would you like to come for the drive.'

Bill stuffed his comic into his trouser pocket with untypical haste, pushed the hair out of his eyes, and said, 'Come on then if you're going.'

'What d'you want to be going back to that shop for?' Marlene demanded, sitting up. 'You was there yesterday.'

'I forgot the sugar,' said Mrs Manders.

'Me and Bill, we don't need sugar. We don't want it. No need to fetch it for us.'

'Afraid Tom does,' said Mrs Manders. 'You can stay here though. Just as you like.'

'Naw,' said Marlene. 'I've got to go haven't I if our Bill's going.'

Jinny shrugged her rucksack impatiently. She was ready to go. She wanted nothing so much as to get away from them all. To get away from her family and most of all to get away from Marlene.

Jinny stared at Marlene resentfully. The enthusiasm that had lit up Marlene's pale face when she had been riding had vanished. As she struggled to her feet, Jinny could see the pinched, withered expression clamped at her mouth and eyes.

'Wait on me, Bill,' Marlene shouted and limped after Bill, who was already striding up the path. 'Wait on me.'

Mrs Manders, speaking more to Sue than to Jinny, hoped that they'd remember to brush their teeth if not their hair and that the sun would go on shining for them.

'The moon will be shining if we don't get a move on,' Jinny muttered as Shantih pranced impatiently at the full length of her reins.

Mrs Manders said goodbye and went up the path after Bill and Marlene.

'At last,' said Jinny. 'At flippin' last.' And, leading the way, she turned Shantih towards the moors. 'We could have been away an hour ago if it hadn't been for her. I don't know what she thinks Shantih is. Some kind of seaside donkey. Always wanting rides on her. Always going on at her the way she does. Stupid nuisance!'

'Marlene's OK,' said Sue, leading Pippen behind Shantih. 'She's just keen. And you never hear her complaining about her leg.'

Jinny snorted. 'She complains enough about Shantih. Always wanting to ride her. Wanted to stand in the field holding the halter. Just stand there holding the halter!'

'I was like that about Pippen.'

'That's different. That's quite different. Shantih could have kicked her or anything. Reared up and kicked her. Marlene wouldn't even have noticed until her head was rolling on the ground. And then what would have happened to Shantih?'

Jinny's bad temper was set, hard and furious. She had to keep on telling Sue how impossible Marlene was, how incredibly stupid, how she had absolutely no right to even touch Jinny's horse.

'Hey, hey there. Wait a minute. You two wait on me. Hey. Wait on me.'

'Oh no!' exclaimed Jinny. 'What does she want now?'

Marlene was running after them with her arms

swimming through the air to help her to keep her balance. She limped right up to Jinny.

'Here you are,' she said, tugging at something in her pocket. 'Nearly forgot, what with all that banging about you made me do. Bashed me brains. Them's for the old horse.' And she thrust a paper bag full of sugar lumps into Jinny's hand, and before Jinny could say anything she was hirpling back to Finmory.

Jinny stared at the sugar lumps in disgust.

'What did she want to give me these for? Shantih doesn't want them!' And Jinny almost threw the sugar away, but something in the way Sue was looking at her made her keep them.

'Stupid thing,' she declared and marched on with Shantih jogging at her side.

The sun blazed down and the flies zooming round Jinny's head made the day seem hotter than ever. The metal frame of the rucksack hurt her back, its straps gnawed into her shoulders. It seemed to grow heavier and heavier at every step she took. She tried balancing it on Shantih's saddle and holding it there as they walked along, but the Arab sprang away and the pack went crashing to the ground.

Sue stood watching, without offering to help, while Jinny tried to hoist the rucksack onto her back again and hold on to her skittering horse at the same time. Sue waited without speaking until Jinny had reorganised herself and then followed on behind her.

*Not going to be much of a camp if Sue's going to be like this*, thought Jinny. She'd given up trying to make conversation. No matter how often she'd pointed out to Sue how hopeless Marlene was, Sue hadn't joined in. As she plodded on, Jinny could feel the bag of sugar lumps in her pocket and hear Marlene's voice telling her to give them to the old horse.

*Old horse, indeed*, thought Jinny. *She is just so stupid. It's a good job I'm taking Shantih away from her.* And she wondered if they could possibly go on camping until the Thorpes went back to Stopton.

As she trudged on, Jinny's mind bubbled and boiled, full of all the things that made her hate Marlene. She had to keep on telling herself how dangerous it was for Marlene to be near Shantih, telling herself over and over again that Marlene was too stupid to ride Shantih, for no matter how hard she tried to block it out she kept seeing Marlene's white pinched face. She couldn't stop herself remembering the dirt and noise of Stopton and the decaying slums where Marlene and Bill lived. Worst of all was the thought of Marlene's delight when she had started to trot, the way she had lit up with excitement.

'You could have steadied Shantih. Held Marlene's leg against the saddle. Shown her how to post. And what did you do? You tried to make her fall off.'

'But she knows nothing about horses!'

Jinny shouted the words inside her head. But it was

too late. She had allowed herself to listen to the voice.

'How could she know about horses?' demanded the voice that was her parents and Ken, and Jinny herself, really. 'There's not many Arabs in Stopton.'

'I'm telling you she could hurt herself,' yelled Jinny in silent self-defence.

The voice that couldn't be silenced now that Jinny had started listening to it laughed scornfully.

'Is that so?' it said. 'How convenient.' And resentfully Jinny knew what she was going to have to do.

'Pippen is sweating like anything,' Sue called. 'Can we have a stop?'

'OK,' said Jinny and collapsed on to a handy boulder.

Sue sat down on the grass. Neither of them spoke. The silence was filled with waiting for who was going to speak first.

'Go on,' urged the voice in Jinny's head. 'It's all your fault. Sue would have brought Marlene with us.' Jinny drew in her breath and said, 'We can't, can we?'

At the same moment Sue looked round. 'Let's go back for Marlene,' she said.

# Six

Shantih and Pippen trotted back side by side to Finmory. The two girls had unloaded Pippen and deposited the rucksack, frying pan and Jinny's sleeping bag on the ground.

'May as well camp here,' Jinny had said. 'It's not too bad a place. Quite close to the burn.'

'It's great,' agreed Sue. 'A wall to shelter us and that old sheep pen to tie the ponies to. And a smashing view. We could never take Marlene all the way to the standing stones.'

'This isn't really very far from Finmory,' Jinny had said regretfully. 'There's a shortcut through Mr MacKenzie's yard, but the last field gate is sometimes locked, then you have to trail back and come round this way.'

As Finmory came into sight, Jinny said, 'I expect

they'll all come and visit us, now that we're camping so close to the house.' She wasn't looking forward to telling Marlene that she was sorry for being so mean, and was trying to keep her thoughts on other things. 'Your parents could come to.'

'They'd like that,' said Sue. 'Mum plays the guitar. She'd bring it with her.'

And Jinny imagined them all sitting round a blazing campfire, singing, while the horses listened, ears pricked, eyes glinting in the firelight.

'I'll hold Shantih,' Sue offered when they reached Finmory. 'You go and find Marlene.'

'Say she doesn't want to come?'

'You know she does.'

'Oh well,' said Jinny and went off to look for Marlene.

There was no one around the stables, no one in the garden, and then Jinny noticed that the car wasn't there.

*Can't be back from Mrs Simpson's*, she thought and drew in a gasp of relief. It would be a few minutes at least before she had to apologise to Marlene. She thought of going back to tell Sue to put the horses in the stable and come in for lemonade but decided not to bother. If she could manage to speak to Marlene without Sue listening Jinny felt it would be easier.

She leaned against the back door, the sun burning down on her. 'Jinny Manders,' she told herself. 'You very nearly ruined your summer holidays too. Just saved yourself in time.' And she went over in her mind what she would say to Marlene.

There was a noise in the kitchen. Too definite to be Kelly or one of the cats. It was a person. Jinny heard them draw back a chair and sit down at the table.

*Ken*, thought Jinny. *May as well tell him first*. She pushed open the back door and ran inside.

Bill was sitting at the table, hunched over something he was holding in his hands. Blinded by the dark kitchen after the bright morning, Jinny couldn't see what it was.

Bill jumped up when he heard her come in, fumbling to hide what he had been looking at behind his back.

'What you want?' he demanded, glaring suspiciously at Jinny.

'Sorry,' said Jinny. 'I didn't mean to give you a fright. I'm looking for Marlene.'

'She ain't here.'

'I can see that,' said Jinny. 'Is she still at Glenbost?'

'Naw. She's out at them vegetables with the hippie,' Bill told her as he backed away.

'Thanks,' said Jinny and went off to Ken's kitchen garden.

She made herself walk steadily – left foot, right foot. Her mind too full of apologising to Marlene to leave any room for wondering why Bill had looked so guilty.

Just before she reached the kitchen garden, Jinny

hesitated behind a screen of rhododendrons. She could hear Marlene's high-pitched voice rasping at Ken.

'We had a little pup once but me Mum got sick of it, messing the floor and eating all her good things. She was having a tea party for her friends, like, and she had it all laid out nice with a fancy cloth covering it all and when her friends came they lifted up the cloth and there were only the pup there. He'd eaten all the cakes and things. Didn't take me Mum long to get shot of him after that. But he were a nice little thing. He were brown with a bit funny tail. Used to push him round in a pram, all tucked in proper nice.'

*Oh no*, thought Jinny. *Days of listening to that; of listening to her talking nonsense and having to watch her ride Shantih.* Then Jinny thought of going back to tell Sue that she had changed her mind.

'Bear up,' she told herself. 'It's only for a day or two,' and she stepped out from behind the bushes.

Marlene was making a daisy chain. Kelly, lying beside her on the grass, was already wearing one round his neck. Ken was standing between his rows of vegetables, the hoe he held in his hands seemed almost to be working by itself, moving slowly but rhythmically. He looked up, saw Jinny, but didn't speak.

Jinny swallowed hard and marched towards them.

'Well, look who's here,' said Marlene. 'You'll be in that book for records, you will. Shortestest camp in the world, that's what you'll be.'

'We've come back for you,' said Jinny. 'Come and camp with us. I'm sorry I didn't ask you before. I thought it would be too far for you.'

'Eh, get her,' said Marlene. Her black eyes glistened without expression in her whitish-yellow face. 'Want me to come running now do you? What's up? Can't neither of you do the cooking?'

'We were going to the standing stones but it was too hot,' lied Jinny. 'So when we decided not to go as far as that we came back for you.'

Marlene went on with her daisy chain.

'Sue wants you to come,' said Jinny.

'Maybe,' said Marlene. 'But what about you? You think I'm not posh enough for your horse, don't you?'

'She doesn't,' stated Ken. 'Things have just got a bit twisted between you.'

'I'm asking you,' said Jinny. 'I wouldn't have come back for you if I hadn't wanted you to come.'

'That'll be it,' said Marlene.

'Go on,' said Ken. 'Don't hold on to that nonsense.'

Marlene grinned quickly at Ken.

'What makes you so sure that I'd want to give up a comfy bed to sleep on dirty old ground, eh? I ain't daft.'

'It'll be fun,' said Jinny. 'An adventure. Something new. Exciting.'

'Exciting!' scoffed Marlene. 'Reckon that's the last thing our lot needs. Anyway, can't go all that trail with me leg.'

Jinny stared at her in despair. She was sure that Marlene could walk over the moor if she wanted to. Jinny wanted to shout, 'All right, then, stay where you are,' but heard her own voice saying, 'You can ride Shantih.'

Marlene's mouth twitched, she kinked a quick look out of the corner of her eye at Ken.

'Need to get me bag,' she said, scrambling onto her feet.

'You won't need it,' said Jinny.

'That I will,' said Marlene.

Jinny went to find Mike's sleeping bag for Marlene to use, then she waited in the garden for Marlene to return with her shopper.

'Didn't they go with Mum and Dad?' Jinny asked Ken.

'To the shop? Yes. They've all been to the village. Think your parents went into the farm and the kids came on here.'

'That's me,' said Marlene, clutching her tartan shopper to her stomach. 'Now mind,' she said to Ken. 'We made it a promise. You keep an eye on him or I ain't going.'

'All the time,' confirmed Ken.

'What?' said Jinny.

'Me brother. Ken there'll watch him while we're up at the camp. We arranged it.'

'You did, did you?' said Jinny, realising that if Ken

87

and Marlene had arranged it they must have been expecting her to come back.

'Knew it wasn't you,' said Ken.

'Nearly was,' Jinny said to Ken. She told Marlene that Sue had been waiting ages for them, and they all went down to join her.

'Right pleased you came back for me,' Marlene said to Sue.

*More than she said to me*, thought Jinny darkly.

'Where is the camp now?' Ken asked. 'Dare say your mother will feel safer if she knows.'

'Not far,' said Jinny. 'By the old sheep pen. That's where we've left the stuff so that's where we'll camp. If you go up the hill for a bit, you'll be able to spot the tent.'

'Bright orange,' said Sue. 'So that helicopters and St Bernards can spy us out.'

'Mind and tell Bill where I'll be,' said Marlene. 'In case he wants me or anything, like. I've told him I won't be gone long.'

'Only a day or two,' said Jinny, taking Marlene's bag while she mounted. 'No. I'll hold it while you're riding. No, I shan't drop it.'

'Take joy,' said Ken, and went back to his hoeing.

'What about the shortcut you were talking about?' Sue asked.

'It's much quicker,' said Jinny, seeing herself battering through bogs and bracken, trying to control Shantih and keep Marlene on top. 'But no,' she decided. 'The gate might be shut and it's so maddening when you have to turn round and come all the way back.'

'Couldn't we jump?' asked Sue.

'On Shantih?' demanded Jinny, feeling her stomach tighten – half nerves, half excitement. 'But I've never jumped Shantih!'

'First time,' suggested Sue.

'No chance,' said Jinny. 'It's a five-bar gate and the walls are built up to keep Mr MacKenzie's cows in. It is *huge*.'

'In that case,' agreed Sue, turning Pippen round the way they had come, 'old man Finnigan begin agen.'

After ten minutes of trying to answer Marlene's questions, Jinny stopped listening to her and Marlene went on chatting to Shantih. Jinny had made a rule. Hold on to the pommel with one hand. She had used her father's no nonsense voice and Marlene was doing as she had been told.

Jinny smiled to herself as she plodded along behind Pippen's brown and white bottom. She could see the moorland again, the shimmer of the sea; the black cliffs, the hazy, summer mountains. They were all part of her again. Instead of hating Marlene, she was alive again, and Jinny glanced up at Marlene to make sure she hadn't abandoned her firm hand hold.

'Eh, this is smashing,' beamed Marlene. 'Even the old horse is enjoying hisself, ain't he?'

Jinny agreed.

Sue pulled Pippen back to ride beside them.

'Have you ever jumped?' she asked Jinny.

'Once,' said Jinny. 'On Clare Burnley's showjumper.'

'Not on Shantih?'

'No! I'm just reaching the stage where I can control her at a canter.'

'There's loads of places here where you could jump,' said Sue, pointing to the low, broken-down walls that crisscrossed the moor. 'We could easily clear away the fallen stones and make a place for jumping. Shall we?'

'Now?' said Jinny in alarm.

'Why not?' challenged Sue.

'Not with me on horse,' cried Marlene and instantly began to dismount. Shantih shied, depositing Marlene on the ground. 'Getting as bad as you,' Marlene said to Jinny. 'Neither of us much good at this old riding.'

'Really!' said Jinny in disgust. 'You've got some cheek!' Then she realised Marlene was laughing at her.

The thought of jumping made Jinny curl up inside. She had read books about training horses to jump and none of them had suggested just suddenly starting to jump over stone walls.

'I don't mean great enormous jumps,' declared Sue. 'Well, if you don't want to jump, I do. Here,' she said to Marlene, 'hold his reins.' She jumped down from Pippen and walked across to the wall.

Jinny, on Shantih, and Marlene, being led by Pippen, followed her across.

'This would do,' said Sue, lifting fallen stones out of the way. 'Good landing. No holes. And that couldn't be too high for anyone.'

Jinny regarded the wall with a measuring eye. If she thought of having to jump Shantih over it, it looked about three feet; if she saw it as just an old wall, it probably wasn't even two feet high.

'Shouldn't we start with a pole on the ground and things like that first?'

'Oh, come on,' said Sue. 'This is fun. Not Hickstead. I'll go first.'

'If she gets too excited I'm not jumping,' said Jinny, feeling her mouth go suddenly dry. She certainly wasn't afraid, but . . .

Sue gathered up Pippen's reins, trotted him in a circle, turned him to face the wall and cantered him straight at it. With a gay flick of his tail, Pippen bounced over.

*Now me*, thought Jinny as she eased Shantih into a slow sitting trot and took her round in a circle. She turned her horse to the jump, and Shantih, her ears pricked, raced at the wall. Jinny was only conscious of a sudden blur of speed, Shantih's neck arching in front of her, her mane blown back; and then, long before Jinny expected it, Shantih had taken off. Jinny jack-knifed over her shoulder, caught a vivid glimpse of

Shantih's white legs tucked up close to her body, and then they had landed, far out on the other side of the wall.

'Whee!' exclaimed Sue.

Marlene clapped her hands above her head and stamped her foot, making Shantih shy and whirl round.

'Nice one old horse!' she shrieked.

Jinny was too delighted to care. Her face had almost disappeared behind its ear-to-ear grin.

Pippen bounced back, popping obediently over the wall, and Shantih cantered behind him. Again she spread herself over the wall in a flowing arc.

'Jump back over again,' said Sue, 'and then we'll try something higher.'

At the other side they searched for a higher bit of wall that was safe to jump.

'That's enormous,' said Jinny in delight.

'Might be two foot six,' deflated Sue. 'Watch her this time. Be ready for her cos she'll really need to jump.' Sue sat down in her saddle and rode Pippen determinedly at the wall. He cleared it with hardly an inch to spare.

Shantih plunged to follow him. Jinny checked her, trotted her in a circle, then, controlling her between her seat and hands, cantered her at the wall. She felt her horse rise up and over, then they seemed to come soaring down as if they had just cleared a steeplechase fence. Jinny was thrown forward when Shantih landed, lost a stirrup but stayed on top.

'That was super,' she cried and threw herself over Shantih's neck, arms outstretched round her, praising her horse.

'Has she really never jumped before?' asked Sue.

'Not with me,' said Jinny. 'She flew over that. I didn't have to make her jump. She wanted to.'

They went on jumping low bits of the wall until Marlene said to give the old horse a chance and when were they coming to this tent because she was starving, so they said now and went on to the campsite. Marlene led Shantih by the reins because she thought she needed a rest and Jinny held on to the halter rope in case a sudden grouse flew up under Shantih's nose or she saw a tiger lurking in the bracken.

As they walked up the hillside Jinny was suddenly aware of walls. They had always been there but she'd never really noticed them before. Now she was looking for places where she could jump; thinking of bringing a can of paint up the hill with her and marking suitable places with splodges of white paint so that she could canter over the moors and jump the walls without stopping to check whether they were safe to jump.

The tent, sleeping bags, rucksack, pan and their other things that had been stacked on Pippen were still lying obediently where they had left them that morning. It seemed to Jinny as if she had left them there in another life. Then she had been thinking about nothing but Marlene and now Shantih could jump. Jinny was lost in a dream of taking Shantih over Badminton-sized fences, over drop jumps and even possibly round the red and white show jumps at the Inverburgh Show next year.

'First thing,' said Sue, 'is to get the tent up.'

Reluctantly Jinny abandoned the applause that followed her out of the ring after Shantih had jumped her clear round.

'Shall I tie him to the fence?' Marlene was asking, and Jinny realised that Sue had taken Pippen's tack off and tied him up to the most solid-looking bit of the sheep pen.

'Aren't you going to tie her up?' Sue asked.

Jinny looked dubiously at the sheep pen's rotted wood. Shantih would never stand tied to that. In fact, Jinny wasn't too sure that Shantih would stand tied to anything in the open.

'Think I'd better hold her.'

'You can't hold her all the time,' Sue said. 'Who's going to help me with the tent?'

'Me,' said Marlene.

'Well, I can't just let her go,' said Jinny, seeing Shantih careering back to Finmory or running wild with Mr MacKenzie's herd of Shetlands.

'What about tonight?' Sue asked. 'You can't hold her all night.'

'But I'll hold her just now,' said Jinny.

# *Seven*

Sue and Marlene put up the tent, arranged the sleeping bags and laid out their food while Jinny, leading Shantih, brought a bucket of water from the burn and gathered dried bracken and heather. She found some flattish stones and laid them in front of the tent to make a fireplace.

'We'll need to go wooding to Loch Varrich,' Jinny said. 'We could light a fire with these bits but we'll need branches to keep it going.'

'What d'you want a fire for?' demanded Marlene. 'Right hot up here. We don't need a fire.'

'For the water,' Jinny told her. 'You can't drink it unless it's boiled.'

'I can,' said Marlene. 'Bit brown, but it's not that bad really.'

'Further up the hill,' said Jinny, 'there might be a

dead fox or a dead sheep lying in that burn and all the water that flows past here has been over it – that's why we need a fire. You can catch terrible diseases drinking burn water if you don't boil it first.'

'Should think I've had them all,' said Marlene, unimpressed by Jinny's warnings. 'You want to see our water. Real green.'

Unwillingly, Marlene agreed to stay at the tent while Jinny and Sue went wooding on their horses.

'You be back before it's dark,' Marlene said. 'Don't want them wolves eating me, do I?'

Jinny rode Shantih as fast as she dared to Loch Varrich, galloping over any flat stretch of moor, keeping at a steady trot even when her horse was stumbling into holes and over hidden stones. Jinny could hear Sue urging Pippen on as they tried to keep up with Shantih but Jinny didn't slow down. She closed her legs against Shantih's sides and forced her on.

'One minute mile?' asked Sue crossly, when they reached the pines above the loch. 'What was all the hurry for?'

'In case the wolves eat Marlene,' replied Jinny, not looking at Pippen's bellowing sides and sweat-streaked neck and trying not to notice Shantih's gulping nostrils Jinny was planning to make her horse so tired that she would be glad to stand tied for some of the night at least.

They gathered dead pine branches, tied them into

bundles and took them back to camp. Sue rode Pippen and dragged her bundles behind her. Jinny clutched Shantih's reins with one hand and the string tied round her branches with the other. She had fallen off twice before Sue had decided that it would be quicker if Jinny walked. As the bundles of wood bounced along, Shantih pirouetted and shied, high trotting in panic at the terrible creatures bounding behind her.

*Good*, thought Jinny. *After all this carry-on she'll not have the strength to break loose.*

Marlene was watching out for them.

'Where you been then?' she demanded. 'I've been that scared, left here on me own. There weren't no noise. Thought it was a trick you were at. Taking the horses and leaving me here. Been much longer I'd have been for off.'

'Blimey,' exclaimed Sue. 'We couldn't have been much quicker.'

'I got a bit bothered about our Bill,' said Marlene. 'Should I go down and look at him, like, and see how he's doing?'

'You can't go back to Finmory tonight,' said Jinny. 'Bill's OK. He's with Ken.'

Marlene looked blankly at Jinny, as if she hardly heard what Jinny was saying, or if she did hear, knew that it didn't matter, and Jinny recognised the look. It was the way she had looked at people when Shantih had been starving on the moor and they kept telling her that the Arab would be all right.

'Just nip down?' pleaded Marlene.

'Goodness,' said Sue, taking Pippen's tack off and leading him to the sheep pen. 'He's older than you, isn't he? I should think he's perfectly all right.'

Jinny hesitated, torn between admitting to herself that she knew what it was like to be worried about something and surrounded by people who didn't understand, and because she knew this, knowing that she had to try and help Marlene; and the more pressing need of deciding whether she could really risk tying up Shantih.

'Tie her up here, next to Pippen,' Sue called. 'This bit here is strong enough. You can't hang on to her all night.'

'I could scoot down,' said Marlene.

'Of course you can't,' Jinny snapped, worried about Shantih. If they'd camped at the standing stones Jinny had been planning to tie her up to a tree that grew close by. Shantih might have pulled against the tree but she couldn't have pulled it up by the roots. Looking at the grey, weather-gnawed wood of the sheep pen, Jinny knew that Shantih could drag herself free from it in seconds.

'I'll wait until later in the evening,' Jinny told Sue. 'She'll settle better then.'

Jinny took Shantih's tack off, rubbed her down and fed both horses from the bag of nuts and oats that they'd brought with them. She would decide later what to do with Shantih. Later was always easier.

Sue was organising Marlene into opening tins and filling the kettle while she blew at the flickering tendrils of flame that bloomed along the dried bracken.

Jinny crouched on the grass, holding Shantih, the Arab looming above her. Shantih's head with its delicate bones, silken skin, great liquid eyes and flimpering muzzle swooped down for a mouthful of oats, then up again, silhouetted above Jinny as her horse stared out over the pearly-grey, luminous space.

*Must be quite late*, Jinny thought. The sun that had blazed above them all day had sunk into a neat, glowing disc touching the distant glint of the sea with one golden finger. The cliffs were smudgy black and the reaches of moor had softened from their sun-chiselled enamel into pastel shadings that glowed more warmly than the greying sky.

Sue placed branches carefully over the core of fire. Tongues of flame licked greedily, crackled and bit, and Jinny smelt the itchy wood smell at the back of her nose. The flames spawned shadows. Suddenly it was almost night. One minute grey, stretching evening, the next minute night.

Shadows had crowded Sue, Marlene and the tent into a centre of golden security. Jinny moved closer to the fire.

'Beans?' said Sue as she tipped baked beans into

the frying pan. 'With sausages and, when Marlene finds them, eggs.'

'Gone proper dark, ain't it,' said Marlene. 'Better get me torch.' She burrowed into her tartan shopper.

'Forgot!' said Jinny.

'Never thought,' said Sue.

'You see,' said Marlene. 'Can't do without me.' She shone the torch to and fro in the dark. 'It's me mum's. She'd have a canary if she could see me sitting out here with her good torch.'

Marlene began to laugh and suddenly they were all laughing – infectious giggling that brought them together and made them all forget that only a few hours ago they'd left Marlene behind.

Still giggling, Marlene found the eggs.

'One day at school,' Marlene told them, 'we had this student teacher and we all had to take a turn round the class at being Noah, getting them all into the ark, like. We had to say, "forward the elephants", or "forward the horses", but you hadn't to say an animal any of them others had said. Well, when it were my turn they'd had all the animals I knew, so I said . . .' Marlene doubled up at the memory. 'I said . . . I said, "forward the eggs!"'

'Forward the eggs,' choked Jinny in delight. It seemed the funniest thing she had ever heard.

Outside the circle of firelight, Pippen clattered the sheep pen, disturbed by the din and Shantih pricked curious ears, staring in uneasy suspicion at the three girls rolling on the ground shouting, 'Forward the eggs!'

Sue ate her meal out of the frying pan because she'd only brought two bowls and there were three of them now. They ate jelly cubes as they waited for the kettle to boil and when it did they drank tea-bag tea and ate wedges of Sue's mother's fruit cake.

Sue held Shantih while Marlene and Jinny washed up in the burn.

'My hands!' cried Jinny, flapping her frozen hands as she tried to bring them back to life. 'I've got burn bite.'

'What a fuss,' said Marlene. 'Where we lived once we only had the one tap and it was always right freezing.'

'But you could boil kettles,' said Jinny.

'Not likely,' said Marlene. 'Them rotters had cut us off.'

'You'd no electricity?' asked Sue incredulously. 'Or gas?'

'We'd bloomin' candles,' said Marlene. 'Didn't even give enough light to scare off them rats.' She flashed quicksilver glances at Sue and Jinny, mocking them.

'Well, anyway,' said Sue a shade too quickly, not believing Marlene, 'what are you going to do with her ladyship? Is she coming into the tent with us?'

'Is there a sleeping bag for her?' countered Jinny.

She had seen the Stopton slums. In her mind she understood that people who lived there had rats in their houses. But she didn't know it. Couldn't believe it really possible. To open a door and see rats in your house.

'Better to tie her up now,' decided Sue. 'While we're still up. She will be all right. Pippen'll keep an eye on her.'

Reluctantly, Jinny led Shantih across to the sheep pen. It was really dark, now that she was away from the fire.

*But there'll be a moon later*, Jinny thought as she tested the wooden bars, trying to find the strongest place. She imagined herself lying warm inside her sleeping bag and being able to look through the flap of the tent and see Shantih.

'Stand quietly now,' Jinny murmured, clapping Shantih's sleek neck. She ran her hand over the mare's withers, stretched her arm over Shantih's back to clap her hard side and quarters, waited a moment leaning against the warm, safe bulk of her horse, then she tied her up with a quick-release knot to the strongest part of the sheep pen.

'You've got Pippen,' Jinny told Shantih. 'You're perfectly safe. Stay there till the morning. I'll be in the tent. You don't need to be afraid.'

Jinny took a few steps away from Shantih and waited. Pippen went back to his dozing, his round bulk tipped to one side by a resting hind leg, his head hanging. Shantih's neck was arched, her head high, sniffing the breeze from the night moors, and Jinny wondered if she might be smelling the Shetlands, wondered if she remembered when she had roamed the hills with them. Shantih stepped back, testing the rope that held her. She whinnied – a shrill, sudden sound – and Pippen wuffled back to her.

*He's telling her not to be so silly*, Jinny thought, as she saw Shantih relax.

'There,' said Sue, coming over to inspect. 'She'll be all right. Stop bothering her. Come back to the fire. Marlene's making cocoa for us. We'll need to get more wood tomorrow, we've nearly used up the lot we brought today.'

Jinny shivered, realising how cold it was away from the fire. She shone the torch beam for a last look at Shantih, trying not to notice the rusty nails sticking out of the planks of wood or the sheets of corrugated iron that still clung loosely, here and there, to the pen. It wasn't the place to tie up a horse and Jinny knew it. Maybe all right for Pippen but not for Shantih.

'Come and get it while it's hot,' shouted Marlene and Jinny went unwillingly over to the fire.

'You're the old cow's tail so you'll need to have the bowl,' said Marlene, handing Jinny a bowl of cocoa. 'But you can have all the sugar you want, nobody here won't be counting.' Marlene gave Jinny the bag of sugar with a spoon stuck in it. 'We're right comfy here, ain't we? Once you brew up you can make any old hole proper nice. That's what me mum says.' Marlene beamed at Jinny. 'Guess I'll be for the old horse again tomorrow, won't I? Can we do some more of that trotting bit?'

Jinny nodded, hardly listening. Her ears were tight to hear the least movement from Shantih. Drinking her cocoa, Jinny was ready to spring up and run to Shantih, ready to grab the tail end of the rope and set her free.

'That bloke Ken – reckon he'll watch our Bill?'

'I'm sure he will,' said Jinny and far below them she heard the wind moan with a low movement of sound.

'It were strange the way he knew you'd come back for me. I were crying a bit when he found me, bit lonely like being left, and he said you'd come back for me.'

Jinny heard the wind again. It came blowing in from the sea, lifting the tent flap, scurrying paper bags they had left lying about, gusting the campfire.

'It's proper knacky that trotting,' said Marlene. 'Guess me wonky leg won't help.'

Sue told her she had known a man with an artificial leg who had hunted, never mind posting.

'Wouldn't want none of that rubbish, killing them little foxes, but I guess I'll need to get this, what d'you call it?'

'Posting,' said Jinny. 'Rising up and down. Stops you bumping about.' But she was listening to the wind, hearing it surging up from the sea, a sudden, howling voice gathering strength as it roared at them over the moors.

'What a wind,' said Sue as the fire smoked and flamed. 'We'll be blown away. And what about Mummy and Dad? They'll be afloat.'

Shantih trampled restlessly back and forward.

*If it's going to be a wild night I'll need to sit up and hold her,* Jinny thought. She zipped up her anorak and stood up to go to the horses.

There was a sudden clattering rattle of corrugated iron, a stampeding panic of hooves and Jinny, running flat out to the horses, saw the whitish gleam of the corrugated iron sheet lifted by the wind. Sue had snatched up Marlene's torch and was running behind her. By its light Jinny could make out the frantic shape of Shantih fighting to escape – her head wrenched upward, the rope taut, her eyeballs white glisters in her head, the skin of her face drawn tight with terror. Her forelegs were splayed out and she pivoted from her crouching quarters as she fought to free herself.

'Pull the end of the rope!' Sue yelled, but already Jinny had ducked past Shantih's straining chest and was tugging at the end of the rope. The pressure of the struggling horse held the knot tight as Jinny jerked it helplessly.

'Can't get it loose,' she screamed, as the sheet of corrugated iron was caught by another gust of wind and flung up again to rattle and crash above their heads.

With a rending, splintering crash, the bar to which Shantih had been tied broke. The mare plunged back, and the rotted lump of wood, still attached to her halter rope, whammed past Jinny, hitting her behind the knees and knocking her down.

'Catch her,' Jinny screamed as she fell. She had seen the rusty nails sticking out of the lump of wood and in her imagination saw the wood entangled in Shantih's legs, the nails ripping and tearing.

'Catch her! Get hold of her!'

As Jinny fought back to her feet she saw Sue grab at the halter rope, miss, and duck away from Shantih's plunging hooves.

'Shantih,' cried Jinny in despair, 'Shantih stop! Stop!'

Then, black against the campfire, Jinny saw Marlene crouch close to the ground, leap up and throw herself at the jolting, leaping, jagged chunk of wood – not thinking of herself first, the way Sue had done, but with a movement so concentrated and direct that she seemed dragged on to the lump of wood as if it had been a magnet. Splayed over the wood, grasping at the rope, Marlene hung on while Shantih plunged above her.

In seconds Jinny reached her, grabbed at the rope, and struggled to calm her horse, to bring sanity back into Shantih's nightmare of terror.

At last the Arab stood still, her flanks heaving, her belly curded with sweat, eyes rolling and her ears pinned back to her neck.

Blood was running down Marlene's face.

'Eh,' she said, 'that were a right to-do. Poor old horse, he don't much fancy being tied up.'

Jinny stared at her, speechless. It was Sue who came to worry about Marlene's face; demanding to know if she was all right; to praise her for holding on to Shantih.

'Weren't you scared?' demanded Sue. 'I was. I thought she was going to kick me.'

'Scared? Me?' said Marlene, dabbing at her face with a grubby ball of paper hanky. 'Not likely. That don't stop me.'

Jinny had unknotted the wood from Shantih's halter and was looking in horror at the twisted nails sticking out of it.

'If she'd gone galloping over the moor her legs would have been torn to ribbons,' Jinny said. 'If you hadn't caught her . . .'

'Eh, but I did, didn't I,' said Marlene and told Sue to stop fussing about the scratch on her face, that it were nothing.

Jinny couldn't speak, couldn't find words to thank Marlene for what she had done.

They all had another cup of cocoa while the wind gusted about them and Pippen, hardly disturbed by all the commotion, returned to his doze.

'I can't tie her up again,' stated Jinny. 'I'll stay up and hold her.'

'We'll take turns,' said Sue.

'No,' said Jinny. 'I'll be OK. She is mine. There's no reason why you should have to sit up.' Sue watched Shantih, who was standing, still fleer-nostrilled and wide-eyed, the wind scattering her mane into wisping strands. Jinny's stomach tightened with love for her horse – the beauty and fire of her. Not for all the world would she have exchanged her for the placid Pippen. But as well as love there was fear, fear that one day Shantih would really hurt someone or damage herself. Jinny imagined her horse's legs torn and bleeding, or Marlene's face if she had fallen on the nails in the wood.

'No,' said Jinny again. 'I'll hold her.'

'Don't be silly,' said Sue. 'Of course we'll take turns. Nothing can happen if we're holding her.'

They argued but Sue won. She held out two blades of grass to Jinny.

'The shortest bit holds first.'

'What about me, then? Suppose I don't matter no more, eh? I'm the only one that was quick enough to catch her. Don't that matter now?'

So they had three pieces of grass. Jinny was first.

'Guess what time it is?' Sue asked when she'd looked at her watch to arrange shifts.

'One o'clock,' guessed Jinny, whose own watch, as usual, wasn't going.

'Quarter to one,' said Sue.

So Jinny took Shantih for the first shift from one to three o'clock. Marlene had drawn second and then Sue was third.

Wrapped in her sleeping bag, her hands inside her anorak sleeves, Jinny held Shantih while the mare grazed. High above them, a wind-scoured moon darted in and out behind billowing clouds. The voices in the tent stopped. The torch was switched off. Jinny and Shantih were alone. Soon it was too cold for Jinny to even think. She waited, frozen, for the hands of Sue's watch to reach three o'clock. At first Jinny decided not to wake Marlene, but Marlene had made her promise and now Jinny wouldn't have cared who she woke as long as she could get in from the cold.

Just before three o'clock Jinny thought she heard someone moving quite close to her. Shantih, too, had looked up suddenly. Jinny swung round, the skin on the back of her neck prickling, but there was no one there. She couldn't see anyone. She tried to listen but the wind made it impossible to make out any movements.

At three, Jinny hobbled on numb feet to wake Marlene. A touch on her shoulder made Marlene spring upright.

'What's up?' she cried. 'What's the matter?'

Then remembered where she was.

'Gone proper perishing,' Marlene said as she

wriggled into the extra clothes she had brought in her shopper.

Jinny waited until Marlene was settled with Shantih, then went back to the tent, too cold to do more than hope they would be all right.

She squirmed down into her sleeping bag, pulling it over her head. Sue was snoring and what felt to Jinny like a force ten gale seemed to be blowing into the tent. She waited, hoping she would fall asleep, but the ground was knobbly and most of the gale seemed to be finding its way into her sleeping bag. Reluctantly Jinny poked her face out into the cold. The flap of the tent was gaping open.

Jinny reached out to tie it together again. Then she looked out for a last check on Shantih.

Her horse wasn't grazing but standing with her neck stretched and her ears sharply pricked. Marlene was holding her halter but paying no attention to her. Jinny had been right. She had heard someone else on the moor and whoever it was they were standing talking urgently to Marlene.

# *Eight*

For a moment Jinny wondered if she should wake Sue. She thought of horror films and night attackers and getting to Pippen so that she could ride for help. But Marlene didn't seem to be afraid. As far as Jinny could make out it looked as if Marlene was holding on to the stranger's arm.

Jinny wriggled out of her sleeping bag and crept out of the tent. Keeping to the pools of shadow by the side of the wall, she moved silently towards Marlene. Shantih saw her. She swung her head round to watch Jinny but Marlene didn't notice the horse's movement. Jinny edged her way closer and realised that the second figure was Bill.

Instantly Jinny felt as if she were spying. Whatever it was that had brought Bill out on to the moors to find his sister had nothing to do with Jinny.

*Say they see me*, Jinny thought. *They'll think I've been standing here listening to them, that I'm the kind of fungus who would want to watch other people when they think they're alone.* Jinny screwed up her face in total disgust.

*Yuch*, she thought and half turned to go back to the tent. A branch cracked beneath her foot. Jinny froze as both Marlene and Bill looked sharply round in her direction.

Jinny waited, her heart leaping in her throat, to be discovered. But although they both seemed to be staring straight at her they obviously couldn't see her and after a moment went back to their discussion. Jinny couldn't make out what they were saying, only the sound of their urgent whispering.

She eased her foot over the ground again, trying to get away before they found her; again the dried heather twigs crackled under her weight.

Jinny held her breath but this time only Shantih heard. Bill was trying to make Marlene take a small, flat parcel and Marlene was pushing it back at him. They were both too involved to have heard Jinny.

Suddenly Bill threw the parcel on the ground, spun round and was off down the hill. Marlene had grabbed at his sleeve but he had been too quick for her. Left alone, she stooped to pick up the parcel and Jinny thought she could see tears glistening on her cheeks.

Marlene walked across to Shantih and stood whispering to the horse, as she looked down uncertainly at the parcel in her hand.

'Right bloomin' idiot,' she was muttering. 'Stupid bloomin' nit.' Then she scrubbed the sleeve of her anorak over her eyes and began to lead Shantih towards the sheep pen.

For a second Jinny thought Marlene was going to try and tie Shantih up again.

*I'll need to pretend that I've just come out to see how she's managing*, Jinny thought, watching anxiously.

But Marlene didn't tie Shantih up. She stopped by the wall at the side of the pen and began lifting down the stones.

*Now's your chance*, Jinny told herself. *Get back to the tent now.*

Jinny took one last look at Marlene working at the wall, then satisfied that, whatever she was doing, she wasn't going to tie Shantih up, Jinny crept back to the tent and crawled into her sleeping bag.

'Is it my turn?' Sue asked sleepily.

'Not nearly,' said Jinny.

'Are you OK?'

'Yes.'

Sue grunted and curled back down. 'Wake me when it's time,' she said and almost before she had finished speaking was asleep again.

Jinny lay flat on her back trying to sort out what

113

she'd seen. She was almost certain that the parcel that Bill had left with Marlene was the same one as he had hidden behind his back when she had surprised him in the kitchen that morning. Why had he brought it to Marlene? What was in it? Why was it so important that he had come over the moors at night to give it to her? Jinny couldn't find the answers.

Before it was Sue's turn to hold Shantih, rain was drumming on the canvas. Marlene's voice woke Jinny.

'Proper pouring,' she said.

Jinny switched on the torch and saw Marlene's rain-sodden hair and pale, wet face looking in at her.

'Better get the old horse home, eh?' stated Marlene. 'No point in hanging about in this?'

Sue emerged to organise an extended halter rope for Shantih made up of stirrup leathers, so they could sit inside the tent holding the end of the halter while Shantih grazed outside.

'Pippen is a very no-trouble pony,' said Jinny, feeling guilty about all the fuss that Shantih was causing.

'Isn't he,' agreed Sue. 'And the thing about him is that he really doesn't mind. He's not just putting it on.' Sue gazed contentedly at Pippen still dozing by the sheep pen, his tail plastered flat over his hocks and quarters by the driving rain.

It was nearly morning and they were all crouched inside the tent, saddles and bridles, rucksacks and food packed in around them.

'I'm asking you,' said Marlene. 'When are we going back down?'

Neither Jinny or Sue were answering.

'We're going to have breakfast soon,' Sue said, consulting her watch. 'Nearly six. We'll have breakfast at six.'

'Then back down?' insisted Marlene.

'It's only a shower,' said Sue irritably.

'Some shower,' said Marlene, and Jinny, looking out at the louring, grey sky and the visible sheets of rain gusting over the moors, had to agree with her.

Pretending to be checking on Pippen, Jinny had taken a quick look at the wall where Marlene had lifted down the stones during the night. At first she hadn't been able to see any signs of Marlene's activities. Whatever she had been doing she had built up the wall again so that no one could tell that the stones had been removed. Then Jinny had noticed several long hairs from Shantih's tail caught between the stones just where Marlene had been standing.

*So I didn't dream it,* Jinny thought and went back quickly to the tent in case Marlene should be watching.

At six they had breakfast – bread and butter, cold baked beans and a tin of peaches. They drank the peach juice instead of water because Jinny refused to let anyone drink unboiled burn water.

'No chance of lighting a fire in this,' said Sue.

'So no one drinks it,' said Jinny flatly.

'When are we going down?' demanded Marlene every few minutes.

'You don't go running home just because it's raining,' Sue told her.

'Do what I bloomin' like,' said Marlene. 'Only loonies sit out in the rain.'

But Jinny didn't think it had anything to do with the rain. She thought that even if the sun had been shining Marlene would have wanted to go back to Finmory to find out what Bill was doing. Jinny hadn't told Sue about Bill's night visit. She wished that she had never seen him herself.

By nine o'clock, Marlene's patience had worn out.

'I ain't waiting no longer,' she announced. 'I got to get back. No use sitting here.' Before Sue or Jinny realised what was happening Marlene was out of the tent.

'Poor old horse,' she said, pausing to clap Shantih's spongy side. 'You ain't half drowned.' And Marlene limped off over the moor.

'Come back,' yelled Jinny. 'You can't go off like that. Come back!'

Hunched over her tartan shopper Marlene didn't even look round.

Sue ran after her. The pair stood in the grey downpour arguing with each other until Sue, her arm round Marlene's shoulders, began to steer her back to the tent.

*Oh well*, thought Jinny. *Home we go.*

She didn't mind. Rain had seeped through her jeans, her feet were sodden, her hair heavy with the rain and her stomach hadn't thought cold baked beans and peaches were the ideal breakfast. To be dry and warm in Finmory kitchen would be quite pleasant, Jinny decided, and with numb hands she began to fumble things back into her rucksack.

'She says she *must* go back *now*,' announced Sue. 'So I suppose we may as well pack up. Looks as if it's going to rain all day. And I don't fancy another night holding Shantih.'

'Next time,' said Jinny, 'we'll need to find something solid to tie her to.'

Shantih's chestnut coat was darkened with the rain. Dark streaks of water ran down her white stockings. It was bad their camp whimpering out like this but it would have been much, much worse if Shantih's legs had been torn by the nails; if Marlene hadn't held on to her. Jinny shuddered at the thought. She looked at Marlene standing in the rain holding Shantih. If Marlene hadn't been there . . . hadn't . . .

'If you'd not caught her last night . . .' began Jinny, desperately wanting to thank Marlene.

'What?' demanded Marlene. 'Eh, don't start on about that now. Come on. Let's get on down quick.'

Marlene's black, bullet eyes glinted in her pale face. She was tense as a coiled spring. Her whole self set on one aim. Last night it had been to hold Shantih. Now it was to get back to Finmory as soon as possible.

Sue loaded up Pippen, tying the soaking tent, sleeping bags, bucket, pans and kettle on to his saddle. Jinny heaved her rucksack onto her back and stared round their campsite, making sure that they hadn't left tins or plastic bags lying about. She scuffled the ashes of their fire, knowing it wasn't really necessary. They were cold and dead with the rain.

It had been good in the evening when they were all sitting round the fire. That had been really nice. But it was over now.

'Eh, come on,' said Marlene.

'Do you want to ride?' Jinny asked her, pulling down Shantih's stirrups, soothing her restless fretting.

'Might as well. Be a bit quicker.' Fingers slipping on the wet leather, Marlene pulled herself into the saddle.

'Thought you'd want to ride,' said Jinny.

'Don't mind. Be quicker.'

'But I thought you wanted to learn to post?'

'Eh, well. Don't matter now. Too late for that. Got to get a move on.' Marlene's knuckles shone through her skin as she gripped the pommel, and from Shantih's back she looked tensely over the moors. 'Gee up,' said Marlene. 'Gee up, old horse.'

Jinny led Shantih down the hillside pushing with all her strength against the mare's shoulder, fighting to control her as she plunged forward, bounding downhill in great leaps that splashed peaty water into Jinny's face. Jolting back and forward in the saddle, Marlene stared straight ahead.

'Don't fuss on about me,' she said. 'Let him hurry up if he wants. Best get out of this rain, ain't we?'

'Doesn't it get boggy?' Sue shouted as Pippen suctioned soup-plate feet through the mire.

'It's the green bits that are dangerous,' Jinny shouted back. 'Suck you down and drown you.'

'Eh, hope our Bill didn't get stuck in one of them,' said Marlene. 'I mean if he were out for a walk, like. He's not used to all this nothing.'

'Hot coffee,' said Jinny as Finmory came into sight.

'Glad to see our tent's still there,' said Sue, looking at the fluorescent patch of colour still perched by the shore.

'Do you want to come up to Finmory?' Jinny offered. 'All of you, I mean.'

'Not likely,' said Sue. 'Dad's got it all fixed up for rain. More like a caravan really than a tent.'

Excited by the sight of home, Shantih broke into a pounding canter. Jinny dug her elbow sharply into her shoulder, yelled at her to behave, grabbed her bit ring and pulled up her head to stop her bucking.

'Stop fussing at him,' ordered Marlene. 'Doing his best to get us back, ain't he?'

So Jinny, splodging at Shantih's side, let the mare surge forward. Marlene's hands were welded onto the pommel and her eyes fixed on Finmory.

*Even if I let go*, Jinny thought, *she'd still be on top when Shantih reached home.*

As they came closer to Finmory, Jinny thought there seemed something strange about the house. No lights in any of the rooms although the morning was dark; no one in the yard or about the stables; no sign of smoke from a fire; not one of her family watching their approach from a window.

*Odd*, thought Jinny, and even as they reached Finmory there was no one to be seen. *Must be the bad weather*, she decided, but knew that couldn't really be the reason. The Manders had lived long enough at Finmory to have stopped staying indoors whenever it rained.

Down past the ruined outhouse they went and into the yard. Still no one opened the door to welcome them. Even when Jinny called, announcing that they were back, there was no reply.

'I'll go on to our tent,' Sue said. 'May as well dump all this clobber. See you later.'

'Right. Come over whenever you like,' Jinny said, but she was thinking how strange it was that all her family should be away from home in the morning. It certainly wasn't the day for a picnic or a drive.

'Let me off here,' demanded Marlene.

'Wait,' said Jinny, 'until we get to the stable.'

'I got to get off now,' cried Marlene, but Jinny

ignored her and let Shantih jog on down to the stables.

The second Shantih reached the stable door, Marlene dropped to the ground. She snatched her shopper from Jinny and began to run back to the house.

'Good job,' said Jinny to Shantih, 'that you've got me to look after you.'

In the loose box Jinny's numb fingers couldn't unbuckle the girth. She put her hand in her mouth, blowing to bring her fingers back to life and then tugged at the buckles again and managed to loosen them. She took Shantih's tack off, fetched an armful of hay for her and then stood pulling the mare's cold, wet ears through her hands to warm her.

'Jinny! Jinny!'

Marlene's voice made Jinny dash out of the stable. It linked with her own uneasy feelings about the strange emptiness around Finmory.

'He's not there,' Marlene cried. 'There ain't no one there. And our Bill's gone. He's taken his case and done a bunk. I shouldn't never have left him to go with that horse.'

Marlene wasn't crying but her face under her rain-flattened hair was peaked and drawn, her mouth twisted into a lipless knot.

'There must be someone in the house,' said Jinny. 'Or a note to say where they are.'

'There ain't,' said Marlene. 'He's gone.'

# Nine

'We're back,' Jinny shouted as she ran along the landing. There had been no one downstairs and no note to say where they had all gone to.

*They wouldn't be expecting us,* Jinny thought, trying to reassure herself. *That's why they haven't left a note.* But she knew that whenever her mother saw the rain she would have been expecting them to come home.

'Anybody there?' called Jinny, her voice echoing through the empty house.

'No need to panic,' Jinny said when she was back in the kitchen with Marlene. 'They've just gone somewhere for the day, that's all.'

'I'm telling you, our Bill's taken his case. That means he's off. And his old books. He ain't coming back, not when he's got his books.'

'There's nothing we can do,' said Jinny. 'We'll just

need to wait until someone comes home. I don't suppose Mike is with them. He hates going for drives. Or Ken.'

'I got to find Bill,' said Marlene.

'How?'

'I don't know, do I? I don't know where to look, not here. I'd know in Stopton. Know all the places he goes there. I'd find him there. I think he's gone back home. That's where he's gone.'

Jinny thought it likely. Perhaps that was what Bill had told Marlene last night – that he wanted to go back to Stopton.

'There's nothing we can do until the others come home,' repeated Jinny. 'You can't go off to Stopton by yourself. We'd better change out of these wet clothes and have some coffee. Shall I lend you a pair of jeans?'

'Got me good ones,' said Marlene, and they went upstairs to change.

When Jinny got back to the kitchen, Marlene was wearing black velvet trousers and a lacy, lurex jumper. She had brought her tartan shopper down with her.

'When's this rain goin' to stop?' she demanded as if Jinny were in control of a rain tap. 'I got to get going. Can't muck about here when Bill's off on his own.'

'Have a cup of coffee,' said Jinny. 'You'll look daft if you go tearing off to Stopton and Bill's only away for the day. Then you'll be in Stopton and he'll be here.'

Marlene considered this while Jinny made the coffee.

'How we going to find out?' she cried. 'I got to know.'

'Don't worry,' said Jinny. 'Surely Bill wouldn't go without you.'

'Not much,' said Marlene. 'Not bloomin' much.'

There was a sound of footsteps outside. Marlene rushed to the door and flung it open. Ken came into the kitchen, his hair sleeked back, his oilskin dripping.

'Hi,' he said.

'Where's Bill?' demanded Marlene. 'Thought you was keeping the eye on him? You let him go off, didn't you?'

Ken hung up his oilskin, asked Jinny if there was a cup of coffee for him and sat down at the table before he answered Marlene.

'Mr MacKenzie phoned up this morning about seven, said he thought we should check up that Bill was OK. He was up with a sick cow and saw Bill going past his farm at about four o'clock. Said he had a case with him. Wondered if we knew.'

Marlene's black eyes stared unblinkingly at Ken as she chewed at her nails.

'We checked Bill's room but he wasn't there. Your Mum and Dad have gone into Inverburgh. Tom thought he might have hitched a lift, trying to get the train back to Stopton. I've been up the moor. Petra and Mike have gone down to the shore, just in case. He might have fallen and hurt himself.'

'Thought you promised,' Marlene accused bitterly.

'You ain't no better than the rest. Thought you understood. I'd have heard him. I'd have stopped him. It's me that's to blame. Shouldn't have gone off with that old horse.'

The sound of a car interrupted Marlene's reproaches.

'That be them?' she cried. 'D'you think they've got him, then?'

Jinny knew that it wasn't their car. It was too powerful.

'Might be news,' she said.

There was a heavy banging at the front door. Jinny went to answer it. A policeman stood there with Mrs Simpson standing behind him.

'Good morning,' said the policeman. 'Is Mr Manders in, please?'

Jinny said he wasn't.

'We'll be coming in to wait on him for it's the urgent word I'm for having with him,' said Mrs Simpson, and, pushing past the policeman and Jinny, she walked into the hall.

The policeman took off his hat, stroked down his sandy hair with a calloused hand and followed the shopkeeper into the kitchen.

'Would you be looking at the state of that one,' said Mrs Simpson, meaning Ken. 'I tell you, Donald,' she said to the policeman, 'they're all tarred with the same brush. Nothing but layabouts has there been in this house since the last of the MacCraes was taken.'

'It's your brother I'm wanting,' she said to Marlene, 'though I daresay you'd be having a hand in it yourself. Be telling me now where's the boy?'

Jinny saw Marlene's shoulders stiffen, her hands clench under the table.

'Do you mean Mike?' Ken asked.

'I mean that one there's brother, as you know very well. The one that stole the watch from my shop yesterday.'

Events linked together like jigsaw pieces in Jinny's mind – Bill in the shop holding Mrs Simpson's eighty-two pound watch; Marlene snatching his hand away from it; their second visit to the shop; the flat parcel Bill had hidden in a guilty fumble when Jinny found him in the kitchen; the same flat parcel he had left with Marlene at their camp.

*And she buried it in the wall*, thought Jinny and sat down suddenly, pretending to tie her shoelace, so that she could keep her head down and stop the kitchen sliding about.

'You ain't got no right to say that. Our Bill never touched your old watch.'

But Jinny knew he had. She felt sick at the thought of it. What good was a gold watch to Bill? Bill would be charged with stealing it but Marlene would be hurt as well. She would feel that it was her fault because she had left him to go camping.

'You could be had up for saying those things about

126

Bill. You ain't got no proof. You're just saying lies to get him into trouble. When me mum hears she'll sort you out. Cos our Bill, he didn't never touch your watch. He didn't have nothing to do with it.'

Words sputtered out of Marlene. Her back eyes darted hate at Mrs Simpson.

'You leave our Bill alone,' Marlene threatened. 'You leave him alone.'

'Would the boy be in the house?' the policeman asked Ken. 'I could be asking him a few questions.'

Ken said no Bill wasn't and the phone rang in the hall. Jinny's feet took her to answer it over a floor that felt as soft as sponge rubber, past walls that breathed in and out.

'Hullo,' she said.

'Jinny,' said her father's voice and Jinny felt tears prick in her eyes, wanted to tell him what had happened but didn't know how to begin.

'Were you washed out?' Mr Manders asked but didn't wait for a reply. 'Tell the others we found Bill at Inverburgh station. Sudden bout of homesickness. He wanted back to the city but he missed the train so he's coming back with us until tomorrow.'

The sound of pips interrupted Mr Manders' voice. 'Sorry, no more change,' he said and the line went dead.

Jinny went back to the kitchen. They all looked round at her, their faces turned on her. She had to tell them.

'Bill was at Inverburgh station,' Jinny said. 'He's coming back with them.'

'Did you hear that, Donald?' Mrs Simpson demanded of the policeman. 'Is that not his guilt clear now! Off to England with my watch.' She stroked her flowered nylon overall down over her knees with both hands. 'And we will be staying here, I'm thinking, until he walks through that door.'

'If you think Bill took the watch yesterday morning,' Ken asked. 'Why weren't you up here yesterday?'

Mrs Simpson regarded him coldly. 'It's no business of yours,' she said, 'but I'll be telling you. Mr Simpson was away on the wee visit to his brother and I was thinking he had the watch with him.'

'He didn't?' asked Ken.

'He did not,' said Mrs Simpson.

Petra and Mike came in and stared in amazement to see Mrs Simpson and a policeman in the kitchen.

'Not surprised,' stated Petra when she understood what was happening. 'He'd been in trouble before, you know. I think it was shoplifting then, as well. Dad'll know. If you ask me they get away with these things once and they just go on doing them.'

*You wait*, thought Jinny, glaring at her sister. *You wait till something like this happens in our family. You'll not be so sure then.*

'Is that a fact, now,' said the policeman, and Ken said that if it was true it was over and done with.

'I'll be telling you this,' said Mrs Simpson. 'I knew there was bad in that boy the minute I saw him. Couldn't keep his thieving hands off that watch. Up to no good. Nothing but a yob.'

'We'll soon be at the truth,' said the policeman soothingly. 'I have the questions ready. Wait now until we see the boy.'

Since Jinny had told them that Bill was coming back to Finmory with her parents, Marlene had sat silently hunched into herself, nibbling at her fingers and picking at a thread in her jumper.

'You don't need to do no more waiting,' she announced suddenly. 'Because I told you, didn't I? It wasn't Bill who took your old watch. It were me. I took it. Me you got to get at. Not our Bill. Me.'

A moment of absolute silence followed Marlene's words.

'I don't doubt you'd the hand in it,' declared Mrs Simpson.

'Where is the watch?' asked the policeman.

'But that brother of yours, he was the one taking it from my counter,' said Mrs Simpson, not believing Marlene.

'You never saw him,' stated Marlene. 'And he don't know nothing about it 'cause I took it, see. You come back up them moors with me and I'll get you the watch. I'll show you where I hid it.' And Marlene stood up, hitching at her good velvet trousers, dragging the kirby grip out of her short hair, opening it with her teeth and jabbing it back more securely. 'Come on with me and I'll get your bloomin' old watch for you.'

Jinny's voice that had been stuck in her throat came out in a croak.

'You didn't take it,' Jinny cried. 'I know you didn't. I saw . . .'

Marlene's hands gripped the edge of the table. For a moment, as she realised that Jinny must have seen Bill giving her the watch, Marlene's face lost its mask and Jinny saw her as she really was – desperately vulnerable, powerless against them and terrified that Bill should be charged with stealing a second time.

For that moment it seemed to Jinny that they were alone in the kitchen and Marlene's true face made the false things vanish. Because she had seen Bill, Jinny had the power to break Marlene, to tell them all how Bill had come up to their camp at night to leave the watch with his sister, how Marlene had nothing to do with stealing it. This time Bill might be sent to a remand home.

*If it were Shantih*, Jinny thought. *If they wanted to take Shantih away from me and shut her up . . .*

Jinny couldn't bear to look at Marlene, yet there was nothing else she could do. To see Marlene as she was now was to know what it was like to live in the Stopton slums; what it was like to come to a strange place and be treated the way Jinny had treated

Marlene. 'Oh no,' cried Jinny to herself. 'No! I didn't mean it.' But the moment was naked. The easy words of polite apology weren't there to cover it up. Jinny had been rotten to Marlene. Words couldn't change that. And Jinny saw Marlene throw herself at the bar of wood ripped from the sheep pen, grab Shantih's halter and hold on. 'Oh no,' cried Jinny, but the words had no sound.

Then the mask slipped back into place. They were back in the familiar kitchen.

Marlene turned furiously on Jinny.

'Shut up!' she shouted. 'Shut up! Don't you come messing me up. This ain't got nothing to do with you, Miss La-di-dah Manders. So you shut up.'

'Officer,' said Marlene to the policeman. 'Come on with me up them hills. I'll show you where it is.'

'And what would a watch be doing out on the hills?' asked the policeman suspiciously.

'They were camping up there,' Petra explained. 'Where were you? By that old sheep pen?' Jinny nodded. 'But Marlene can't walk all that way,' continued Petra. 'She's got a bad leg.'

'I ain't a bloomin' cripple,' spat Marlene, putting on her soaking anorak. 'That's me ready. Come on.'

The policeman hesitated.

'Have I to be going myself?' demanded Mrs Simpson.

'Hadn't you better wait until Dad gets back?' suggested Mike.

'Naw,' said Marlene. 'Come on with me now.'

The policeman settled his hat back on his head. 'Does the lassie know the way?' he asked.

'I'll come with you,' said Ken, but Jinny, catching his eye, shook her head at him. She had to tell Ken what had happened. There must be some way of stopping Marlene taking the blame for Bill's stealing. And if anyone could help her Ken could.

Realising that Jinny didn't want him to go with the policeman, Ken asked Mike if he would go and reluctantly Mike agreed.

'A wee bitty thing her age,' clucked Mrs Simpson with satisfaction when the policeman, Marlene and Mike had set off. 'Who would have thought it. Though I'm telling you that nowadays the lassies are as bad as the boys.'

'I know,' agreed Petra. 'The things some of them do at our school.'

Jinny hurried Ken out of the room.

'The pottery,' he said, and impatiently Jinny followed him into the pottery. Its window looked out on to the hills at the back of the house. The rain had changed to a smirring drizzle and through its grey mist Jinny could see the three shapes walking up the hill, heads down, shoulders hunched against the rain. Mike was taking them up the hill the way they had ridden to their camp.

'It wasn't Marlene,' Jinny told Ken. 'It was Bill. He brought the watch up to her during the night. She hid

132

it up there. She's only saying she took it to protect Bill.'

Ken listened to the details.

'We've got to get the watch back to the shop,' he said. 'Make the Simpsons believe that it wasn't stolen.'

'But how? If Marlene takes the stones off the wall and the watch is there, they'll never believe that it wasn't stolen. We've got to take it away before Marlene gets there. But how?' Jinny cried.

She didn't really know about courts or Children's Panels but she pictured Marlene, in her lacy jumper and good trousers, standing in the witness box telling the jury how she had stolen the watch, her bitten fingers clutching the rail of the box, her bullet eyes defying them – not caring what they did to her as long as they left Bill alone.

'They'd guess what you were up to if you rode past them.'

'Marlene would,' said Jinny, and suddenly she thought of the shortcut, the way through Mr MacKenzie's farmyard, on over his fields and out on to the moor. If the gate wasn't padlocked.

'I could try the shortcut,' Jinny cried. 'I'd make it that way.' And she knew she had to try. The gate had to be open. That way she could take the watch out of the wall before Marlene got there.

'Right,' said Ken. 'I'll go after them and do my best to slow them down.'

They raced out of the house together. Ken turned to

run up the hill. Jinny tore through the garden and down to the stables. She grabbed up her tack from where she had left it to go with Marlene. Shantih clattered her box door, expecting to be taken out to her field.

'It's for Marlene,' Jinny explained as she put her bridle on, slid the saddle on to her back and tugged up the girth. 'We've got to get there first.'

In the yard, Shantih flung herself away from Jinny as she tried to mount.

'Whoa, steady, stand still,' Jinny pleaded.

She sprang up, threw herself over the saddle and wriggled upright. Shantih plunged and reared but Jinny hardly noticed. She turned Shantih's head towards the path that led to Mr MacKenzie's farm, kicked her heels against the mare's sides and sent her on at a splattering canter.

Shantih caught Jinny's urgency, knew that this was no ordinary ride, and Jinny felt her respond willingly, with a blithe eagerness that matched Jinny's own determination to reach the wall first.

Sprays of muddy water flew up from Shantih's hooves as she galloped down the path to the farm. Jinny swung her round into the farmyard and saw to her relief that there was no sign of Mr MacKenzie. Only his wife pulled aside the lace curtain of the farmhouse window to see what was causing the disturbance, but by the time she came hurrying to the door Jinny was across the yard and out of sight.

The gate into the first field stood propped open. Jinny crouched over Shantih's withers as they galloped through and flared over the field. She didn't know where her own body ended and her horse began. The piston beat of Shantih's hooves was the beat of her own heart.

'Let the gate be open,' cried Jinny, mouthing the words. 'Oh please, please, let it be open.'

# $\mathcal{T}en$

Shantih galloped across the last field before the gate. The ground was more broken here and Jinny eased her horse to a steady canter as she rode towards a rise in the land. From the top of the slope Jinny would be able to see the gate.

*It must be open. It MUST,* thought Jinny desperately. She hadn't allowed herself to consider what she would do if the gate was shut.

As Shantih cantered the last few strides to the crest of the hill Jinny screwed her eyes shut. At the top of the hill she opened them. For a split second she was still sure that the gate was open, she had seen it so clearly inside her head, but instantly she knew that it was shut. She made a gulping, strangled noise in her throat and thought, *don't let it be padlocked,* as Shantih plunged downhill towards it.

The padlock was made of whitish, blue-grey metal. It held together the links of a stout chain that encircled the gatepost and the gate, and it was locked.

In front of the gate Shantih whirled and fretted. Excited by her wild gallop, she refused to stand still. Jinny had gone cold inside. Had stopped feeling anything. She just didn't know what she could do now.

The gate was a strongly built, five-bar gate. On either side was a four-foot stone wall. At intervals, upright iron bars had been driven into the top of it and three strands of barbed wire strung through them. There was no way for Jinny to get Shantih through to the other side. If she left her horse here and ran to the sheep pen Jinny was certain she would be too late. All the time she had been galloping she had felt the approach of Marlene, the policeman, Mike and Ken; had tried to guess where they would be; how far on they were; had thought of the gold watch lying inside the wall, drawing the others and herself towards it as if it were a magnet; and now they would reach it and she wouldn't.

But there was one way. One way she could reach the watch before Marlene. Jinny hadn't dared to think about it until now.

She could jump the gate.

Jinny sized up the jump. The gate was about four and a half feet high but appeared lower because of the high barbed wire on either side.

'Shantih could jump it,' Jinny told herself.

'But she's never jumped anything like that height. She's hardly ever jumped anything. Nor have I. Not really,' Jinny pleaded with herself. She had done her best. It wasn't her fault the gate was locked. She'd tell the police how Bill had left the watch with Marlene. They'd question Bill, find out for themselves and nothing would happen to Marlene. But Jinny knew that if they sent Bill to a remand home it would be worse for Marlene than anything they could do to her.

She had to jump the gate. There was no other way.

'We've got to get to the other side,' Jinny told her horse. 'You've got to jump it. You can do it easily, easily.'

She cantered Shantih in a circle. Her legs seemed loose against the saddle and a hard choking lump somewhere inside her was stopping her breathing properly.

*I'll hold on to her mane*, Jinny thought, *and then I'll be all right.*

She turned Shantih and rode her at the gate. To Jinny's magnifying eye it seemed to have grown to an enormous size. She crouched stiffly in the saddle, a lump of mane knotted between her fingers.

'Jump!' she shouted at Shantih. 'Jump!' But Jinny's mind was filled with the thought of Shantih hitting the gate, crashing down and lying unable to get up because her leg was broken.

'Jump,' cried Jinny again as she clung nervously to Shantih's mane. 'Jump it!'

Shantih slid to a halt in front of the gate. Her eyes rolling, her tail switching, she swung round and charged away. Jinny grabbed up her reins, hauled her round and rode her at the gate for a second time.

Jinny's voice said words that were meant to urge her on but Shantih only heard her nervous, high-pitched tone. Jinny's clinging hands and rigid body held her back. Shantih stopped dead in front of the gate and Jinny went on thumping into it.

*We're going to be too late*, Jinny thought as she remounted.

*Are you afraid?* she asked herself and knew that the answer was yes. She was afraid.

'Then be afraid,' said the voice in Jinny's head. 'Be afraid but don't let that stop you.' Jinny remembered the look on Marlene's face before she had ridden Shantih for the first time. Marlene had been afraid then but it hadn't stopped her. *And now,* Jinny thought, *telling them she stole the watch, she's afraid of what they'll do to her. And she was afraid when she caught Shantih but it didn't stop her.*

Jinny took off her hard hat, shook her hair back and settled it more firmly on her head. This time she would jump the gate. This time Shantih wouldn't refuse.

Jinny gathered up her reins, steadied her horse, cantered in a circle then rode her at the gate for a third

139

time and this time Jinny wasn't thinking about holding on to Shantih's mane, or of Shantih falling. The only thought in Jinny's head was to be on the other side. Sitting tight in the saddle, Jinny drove the Arab at the gate, left no doubt in Shantih's mind about what she was to do. Jinny held her together, waited for the moment when Shantih must soar into the air if she was to clear the gate safely, kicked her on at that exact moment and Shantih leapt from her hocks, struck upwards, sailed high over the gate and landed far out on the other side.

'You did it!' cried Jinny. 'You jumped it! Oh horse! Horse! Horse!'

As they galloped on, Jinny glanced back once to see a rather low gate just being there between the walls, totally unperturbed by all the commotion, then she set herself to ride as fast as she could to the sheep pen.

Tensely, Jinny searched the moor, knowing where the others would first come into sight, but there was no sign of them, no crows flew up cawing a warning of their approach.

Jinny reached the sheep pen, threw herself off Shantih and searched the wall for the chestnut hairs from Shantih's tail. She found them and began to topple the stones to the ground. She had to remove about a dozen stones before she found the parcel. A plastic bag was wrapped round the box, but the long, flat shape of the box was unmistakable. Jinny grabbed it up and stuffed it into the pocket of her oilskin. She lifted the stones back on to the wall, scraping her knuckles in her haste to rebuild it and be away. A gull rasped the moorland silence with a harsh cry. Jinny froze. What would she say if they caught her? Then she realised that it was only a bird and went on struggling to make the stones balance on top of each other.

You could tell, Jinny thought, surveying the wall, but you couldn't be certain it had been a person. A sheep could have rumpled it. She jumped back onto Shantih.

Jinny didn't stop galloping until she was absolutely certain that she was well out of sight of the sheep pen, then she stopped Shantih and sat slumped in the saddle, took her feet out of the stirrups, dropped her reins. They had done it! Shantih and herself.

'"My horse without peer,"' quoted Jinny, achievement overflowing in her. 'Leaned, patted her ear, called her my Shantih, my horse without peer,' she cried, throwing herself over Shantih's neck, clapping her, praising her.

When Marlene got to the wall there would be no watch for her to find. Mrs Simpson and the policeman would be annoyed, thinking she had tricked them, but Marlene would be safe.

Jinny sat up and took the watch out of her pocket. She put one arm through Shantih's reins to stop them vanishing over her head while she was grazing, and then Jinny unwrapped the box. She opened it and looked at the watch. It seemed to Jinny a clumsy lump of metal, a single handcuff. She shivered, closed the box, wrapped it up again and put it back into her pocket. Now she had to get it back into Mrs Simpson's shop where it belonged.

Without a second thought, Jinny rode Shantih at the locked gate; grinned with delight as her Arab soared effortlessly over it and cantered on to the farm.

Jinny avoided the farmyard. Even if Mr MacKenzie wasn't there, Jinny felt that Mrs MacKenzie would be more prepared to pounce. She walked Shantih down the edge of a sown field, by the side of a wall that bounded a hayfield, and then trotted her out onto the road to Glenbost.

She had to get the watch back before the policeman had the chance to question Bill. From what Jinny knew of Bill she had no confidence in his being able to outwit even the Glenbost police force.

As she rode she eased the watch out of its plastic wrapping. Jinny wasn't too sure how she was going to get it back to the Simpsons but there was a chance that if she lingered over the shop's pile of paperbacks, Mr Simpson, who would be in charge while his wife was at Finmory, would leave her alone while he attended to another customer.

'Need to find someone to hold you,' Jinny told Shantih as the shop came into sight.

Dolina, who had attended the village school and

was going with Jinny to the new Inverburgh
Comprehensive in September, was standing in front
of the garage.

'Is it the mud pack you've been giving her?' Dolina
asked, coming to meet them.

Jinny dismounted. 'Looks like it,' she agreed, seeing
Shantih's mud-splattered legs and sides. 'Could you
hold her for me? I've got to go into the shop.'

Dolina regarded Shantih warily. 'If she's at her
nonsense I'll let her go,' she stated.

'She'll be fine,' said Jinny. 'She'll eat the grass. Don't
think I'll be long.' She handed Shantih's reins to Dolina
and hurried into the shop.

There were two women at the counter. Jinny knew
them both by sight, the way she knew everyone in
Glenbost. They both looked round at Jinny who was
sure that they could see into her pocket and would
think that she had stolen the watch.

'And what can I get for you?' Mr Simpson asked in
a distant polite voice. Normally he teased Jinny about
her red hair.

'I want a book,' Jinny said. 'Can I have a look?'

'Don't be soiling them, now,' Mr Simpson cautioned
and went back to his other customers.

Jinny rubbed her dirty hands down her wet oilskin,
then dried them on her jeans.

There were about twenty children's paperbacks
sitting next to a pile of murders, westerns and romances.

Jinny looked through them slowly. Mr Simpson resumed his conversation with the two women and Jinny, pretending to be reading one of the books, let her gaze wander round the shop. In front of the counter, quite close to the perspex case of watches, was an open crate of apples. It wasn't absolutely underneath the watches, but close enough to make it possible for the gold watch to have fallen in amongst the apples from the top of the case.

*But*, thought Jinny sharply, *the apples would have had to be there before Mrs Simpson noticed that the watch was missing or it couldn't possibly have fallen amongst them.*

Jinny tried to remember if the apples had been there when she had bought their camping supplies. At first she wasn't sure. She could picture them there, or not, whichever way she chose. Then she remembered her father filling a bag with apples from the crate before Mrs Simpson weighed them. The apples had definitely been there on Thursday.

Jinny slid her hand into her oilskin pocket. The box was closed. When it had been sitting on top of the case the lid of the box had been fitted on to the back of the box to display the watch. Still pretending to read her book, Jinny opened the box in her pocket and fitted the lid onto the back.

One of the women went out, which made Jinny start guiltily.

*I should have fixed the box before I came in*, Jinny thought and wondered what other stupid mistakes she had made.

When the box felt all right Jinny palmed it up into her sleeve; holding it there, secret and hidden by her oilskin, while she waited for her chance to put it into the box of apples.

Another woman came in and Mr Simpson began to serve her. She asked for butter and Jinny knew he would have to go into the back shop to take her pound of butter from the great mound that was kept there.

Still reading her book, Jinny moved across to the counter. Mr Simpson went into the back shop, leaving the two women gossiping together. Jinny balanced her book on the very edge of the counter, put her right hand into the right-hand pocket of her oilskin and held out her unbuttoned coat so that the women couldn't possibly see what she was doing with her other hand.

Jinny tipped the book so that it fell to the floor. The women glanced in her direction then paid no more attention to her. Jinny crouched down, still shielding her left hand with her coat as she placed the watch delicately amongst the apples. Then, without looking at the women, she made sure that the fruit was covering the watch. She picked up her book and stood up. Her hands were shaking so much that she had to let the book flop on the counter and bury her hands out of sight in her pockets.

Jinny let her eyes flick down over the crate of apples. The watch was almost completely hidden. Only a tiny patch of its red box was visible. Yet to Jinny it seemed the most obvious thing in the whole shop, as if anyone coming in would instantly stop and point to it, asking what on earth a gold watch was doing in a crate of apples.

*Now to make Mr Simpson find it*, Jinny thought. Everyone must know that the watch had been recovered before the policeman had a chance to question Bill. Jinny drew in long slow breaths, let the air flow slowly out of her nose, as she tried to calm herself.

'Have you decided, then?' demanded Mr Simpson when the two women had left the shop. 'Is this the one you're taking?'

'Yes please,' said Jinny. 'And could I have a pound of eating apples?' To her relief her voice sounded as it always did; as if it was an ordinary day and she was just shopping for her mother.

'You'll have heard about that boy you have with you stealing the gold watch from us,' said Mr Simpson, coming to the front of the counter to fill a paper bag with apples.

Jinny said yes she had.

'It's the sorry day when you've strangers on your doorstep bringing thieves into your shop.' Mr Simpson had put three apples into the bag and was going back behind the counter without noticing the watch.

'Do I only get three?' cried Jinny in alarm. 'Could you make them small ones, please? Could I have four or five small ones, please?'

Mr Simpson glared at her sourly but he tipped the three apples back into the crate and began to hunt around for smaller ones. The movement of the apples pushed the watch to the surface.

Mr Simpson swore in Gaelic as he grabbed it up.

'If it isn't the very watch the boy stole,' he exclaimed. 'Was it yourself put it there?'

'If you say Bill stole it, how could I have put it there?' Jinny said indignantly, hoping she was looking sufficiently surprised. 'It must have fallen. Dropped down and got mixed up with the apples.'

Mr Simpson's eyes totally disbelieved her.

'I bet you're glad to have it back. Is it OK?'

As Jinny left the shop, Mr Simpson was on the phone to Finmory, telling his wife that the watch had been found.

When Jinny got back to Dolina and Shantih she couldn't stop shaking. She leant over Shantih's withers and shook. Her teeth chattered and her hands twitched.

'Are you feeling fit?' asked Dolina.

'Having one,' said Jinny.

Her legs weren't strong enough to get her back onto Shantih.

'I'll walk beside her and lean,' Jinny said, refusing Dolina's offer of a hoist on.

Gradually, as she walked back to Finmory, Jinny began to calm down. She shared the apples with Shantih as they went along.

*Shoplifters should get medals*, Jinny thought. She was feeling as exhausted as if she had been galloping for hours on a runaway Shantih.

First the police car, with Mrs Simpson sitting next to the policeman and staring straight ahead, passed them, and then the Manders' car, with Bill in the back, drove up and stopped beside her.

'Jinny,' said her mother in a surprised tone of voice. 'Are you all right?'

'Perfectly,' said Jinny. 'We were rained off so I thought I'd go for a ride.'

'But you're not,' said her mother. 'Where's Sue and Marlene?'

'Her tent and our kitchen, I should think, and I am having a ride, only at this particular moment I'm not.'

'I see,' said her mother. 'Bye then,' and they drove on.

It wasn't until her parents had driven up and Jinny had seen Bill slouching in the back seat that she had given a thought to the rights and wrongs of covering up for Bill when, after all, he had stolen the watch. Until that moment all Jinny had been thinking about had been stopping Marlene taking the blame.

Jinny knew that Ken would think that for anyone – Mrs Simpson or Bill – to own a watch that cost eighty-two pounds, when human beings were dying because they hadn't enough to eat, was so disgusting that it didn't matter who took the watch. But Jinny wasn't so sure what her parents would think. Her father might feel that Bill shouldn't get off without some form of repayment for all the trouble he had caused. It was, Jinny decided, one of the things that it might be better for her parents never to know about.

It was easier to think about Shantih. Jinny swung herself back into the saddle and, letting Shantih walk on at her own pace, she relived the thrill of sailing high, wide and handsome over the gate. The more she thought about it, the higher the gate became.

*Next autumn the White City and then the Olympics,* thought Jinny, wondering what she would call Princess Anne when they were riding together in the British cross country team, and she laughed aloud at herself.

They were all having a late lunch when Jinny got back. Ken looked up when she came into the kitchen, and Jinny signalled to him that she had managed it. Marlene, as silent as Bill, was bent over her bowl of tomato soup.

'Where have you been?' cried Petra. 'Mrs Simpson and I thought another one of you had run off.'

'Mrs Simpson said you were in the shop when her husband found the watch,' Mike said, wanting to know the details.

'It had fallen into a crate of apples,' said Jinny. Marlene's beady eyes chiselled into her, but twitched away if Jinny tried to look directly at her. 'And I was buying apples for Shantih, so he found it.'

'You'd think they'd have found it before today,' said Petra. 'Lots of people must have bought apples before you.'

'It had sort of worked its way down between them,' said Jinny, and her father said that one thing certain was that they wouldn't leave it on top of the case again.

When she had finished her lunch, Jinny went up to her bedroom. She shut the door firmly behind her. She felt like being alone. She took out a drawing pad and pencil and sat on the floor opposite her mural, thinking that she might do some drawings of Pippen for Sue but she couldn't even start. The pencil in her hand was a dead lump of wood and lead.

Jinny stared up at the mural of the red horse. It had been on the wall before the Manders had come to Finmory and often Jinny wondered who had painted it. The horse's yellow eyes blazed light. It was a nightmare that came charging through the blue green foliage of Jinny's wondering.

'What could it be like?' she wondered. 'To love someone else so much that you said, "do it to me, not to him".'

Footsteps came along the landing towards Jinny's attic stair. She heard them pause, then limp slowly up towards her. Marlene's clenched fist banged on the door.

# Eleven

Jinny opened the door and Marlene limped in. She stood staring round the room.

'Eh,' Marlene said. 'You're a lucky thing, having a place like this for yourself. You ain't half spoilt, you ain't.' Marlene sat down on Jinny's bed. ''Spect you took it. Come on, tell us.'

'I rode Shantih round by the shortcut,' said Jinny. 'And took the watch out of the wall. Then I put it in the crate of apples when Mr Simpson wasn't looking.'

'What you want to do that for? Wasn't none of your business.'

'It was,' cried Jinny. 'I saw Bill bring it up to you last night. I didn't mean to spy on you. I thought he was a stranger and I was coming to see what he wanted and then I couldn't get away. That's how I knew you hadn't done it.'

'He was scared they'd find the watch on him. That's why he left it with me. Thought they wouldn't search me. Said he'd tell them that he knew nothing about it. But see our Bill, he's proper soft. The minute they started with those questions he'd be in a mess.'

'I couldn't let you take the blame for something you hadn't done. I'd have told them it was Bill, only I knew you didn't want that either. The only thing I could think of was to get there first and take the watch back to the shop.'

Marlene was fiddling with the fringe of Jinny's bedspread, plaiting it into little pigtails that sprang out as soon as she let go of them.

'Thanks,' she said without looking up. 'They might have put him away this time.'

'I didn't do it for Bill,' said Jinny. 'I just didn't see why you should say you had stolen it when he did it.'

'Like I love him,' suggested Marlene. 'Not what he does, not what he looks like – same as me, bit of a mess. But he's OK. He's Bill. Me mum's right fond of him too. Thinks the world of him, she does. She don't believe he does any of these things. Thinks he wouldn't steal nothing, not if you dropped a thousand pounds at his feet. She thinks our Bill would hand it in.'

'I bet he would,' said Jinny sarcastically.

'What do you know about it?' demanded Marlene, turning on Jinny. 'You just keep your mouth shut because you don't know nothing about how it really is, you don't.'

Jinny felt her skin creep, a cold shiver run over her scalp. It was true. She lived wrapped round in layers of cotton wool. It had all been an adventure to her. If Bill had gone to a remand home it wouldn't really have made any difference, not to her, not to her safe, secure little world.

'So you keep shut up,' warned Marlene again.

'Of course,' said Jinny. 'I wouldn't tell anyone.'

'Not that sister of yours.'

'Ken knows.'

'Argh, that don't matter. But mind, no one else.' Marlene stood up. 'Best be going to say goodbye to the old horse,' she said.

'Goodbye?' echoed Jinny. 'It's only Friday. You've got another week. Don't you want any more rides?'

'Naw,' said Marlene. 'Too late. We're for the off tomorrow.'

'Not you,' exclaimed Jinny. 'Bill's going but you don't have to go.'

'Not much,' said Marlene scornfully. 'I'm for Stopton tomorrow. Can't let him go off without me.'

'But can't your mother meet him?' argued Jinny. 'You can't spend all your life looking after Bill.'

But Marlene wasn't listening to her.

'Just say tar-rah,' she said as she went towards the door, 'and that'll be that.' Then she stopped and

153

looked through the archway into the other half of Jinny's room.

'Proper art gallery you got here, ain't it,' said Marlene and she went through to look at Jinny's pictures that were pinned on the wall opposite the mural.

Reluctantly Jinny followed her through. She hated other people looking at her drawings. Couldn't bear the things they said, even when they were trying to be pleasant. Once, years ago, her mother had made her show some of her drawings to a friend, the friend had said how nice it was for Jinny to have such a happy hobby. The phrase had stuck in Jinny's mind – always there when Jinny made a mess of a drawing.

'Did you do them? The big one and all?' demanded Marlene.

'Not the mural on the wall,' said Jinny. 'But the rest.'

'Eh-h-h-h!' Marlene let out her breath in slow admiration. 'That's Shantih, ain't it? That's smashing, that is. Eh, that's proper smashing.'

She stood staring at a painting that Jinny had done for a competition.

'See, d'you know what I'd have done if I'd been like you?' Marlene turned her bright face on Jinny, her eyes sparkling, her mouth smiling. 'Like you've drawn Shantih, well I'd have written it. Did a composition about the old horse. Before I knew, like, and it made me feel real happy. As if I was going in on a Saturday night and finding them all settled round the fire. Me dad there too, and Bill, and me mum cooking something up for us all.'

And suddenly Jinny remembered Marlene's composition that her father had shown her before the Thorpes arrived.

'You see,' went on Marlene, 'I didn't know then about all the fuss you have with this riding business. I thought you just sat on like a chair and that were it. Eh, didn't know much then, did I? Thought me leg wouldn't matter, that I'd just sit there and gallop off. Fast, like I can't with me leg.'

'But it is like that,' Jinny cried out. 'Once you've learned.'

'I were scared at first, but once I was on it were OK. Felt like I knew the old horse, somehow. Having written about him and all.'

'But you've done very well,' cried Jinny. 'Lots of beginners would never have gone near a horse again after the way Shantih bucked with you. You only need a bit of practice.'

'Don't have time for that,' stated Marlene. 'Got to go back to Stopton.'

'You don't!' raged Jinny. 'Of course you don't! You can stay and I'll teach you to ride. I will. I promise. Just because Bill wants you to go back you don't need to. They can't do any more about the watch now.'

Marlene shook her head. 'Be proper good,' she said, 'but I ain't staying.'

Jinny listened as Marlene's footsteps limped down the stairs.

*But it's not fair*, she thought. *Why shouldn't Marlene stay? She can't spend all her life looking after Bill. If he wants to steal things, that's what he'll do, whether Marlene is there or not.*

Jinny wondered if she should follow Marlene down to Shantih's field and try again to persuade her to stay, but reluctantly she supposed that it wouldn't make any difference. If Bill went back to Stopton Marlene would go too.

Jinny sat down, picked up her pencil and got on with drawing Pippen.

*Happy hobby*, she thought when she had finished. Her drawing might have been any plump, skewbald pony. It didn't look the least bit Pippenish. Jinny tore the sheet off her pad, screwed it into a ball and threw it furiously into the corner of the room.

'It's so unfair,' she said. 'Why shouldn't Marlene stay if she wants to.' But Jinny knew that if Bill left, Marlene would too.

'I've got to make Bill stay,' cried Jinny. She jumped to her feet and clattered downstairs in search of him.

Petra said no she hadn't seen him but had Jinny tried Mrs Simpson's?

Mr Manders and Ken were loading their kiln and were not pleased at being disturbed. They hadn't seen Bill either.

'Well, I can't tell you where he'll be,' said her mother, 'but I can tell you what he'll be doing. He'll be reading his comics. When we found him at the station he was sitting in a waiting room reading them. What did you want him for?'

'Just something,' said Jinny.

She met Mike carrying full cans of milk from Mr MacKenzie's.

'Seen Bill?' she asked him.

Mike shook his head. 'What were you up to this morning?' he asked.

'Getting back from our camp,' said Jinny, wondering suddenly if it should have been her turn to fetch the milk.

'I mean after that,' said Mike. 'While I was having to trail over the moors with that policeman and Marlene. What were you doing then?'

'Went for a ride,' said Jinny, edging away from her brother. 'I didn't want to stay there with Mrs Simpson and Petra.'

'And,' persisted Mike, 'I think it's very odd the way you just happened to be buying apples when Mr Simpson found the watch in amongst them. That's what I think.'

'Don't think too hard,' warned Jinny.

'Tell me,' said Mike.

'Some day,' said Jinny, grinning at her brother, knowing that he would leave it at that, wouldn't go prodding and prying. Some day she would tell him. Show him the gate that Shantih had jumped.

'Look for Marlene, if you want Bill,' Mike suggested as he walked on to the house.

*Of course*, thought Jinny and ran down to the ponies' field.

Bill was standing by the gate with a comic in his hand. Marlene was in the field feeding bits of bread to Shantih.

'Come and help me clean Shantih's tack,' Jinny called to Bill.

'Naw,' said Bill.

'We're going to clean Shantih's tack,' Jinny called to Marlene. 'We'll be in the stables.'

'I'm not,' said Bill.

'I want to talk to you,' said Jinny, lowering her voice so that Marlene couldn't hear.

'What you at?' asked Bill.

'Come on,' said Jinny and led the way back to the tack room. Bill followed her, unwillingly.

Jinny hung up Shantih's bridle from a hook, found a sponge and a bucket half full of oldish water and began to wipe down the bridle. Through the open door Jinny would be able to see Marlene approaching.

'What?' asked Bill, leaning against the saddle horse. 'What?'

Jinny tossed back her hair, dragged the sponge down the leather with all her strength.

'You're not going back to Stopton tomorrow,' she said. 'Marlene wants to stay until your fortnight's up. She wants to learn to ride. If you go she'll go with you. She won't stay here and let you go. So you're not going.'

'Am that,' said Bill.

'Please,' said Jinny. 'For Marlene. Don't be so mean. You can easily stay for a few more days, only another week.'

'Naw,' said Bill and opened his comic again.

Furiously Jinny snatched it from him and threw it on the ground. Bill swung his fist at her. Jinny ducked and felt the rush of air over her head as he missed her.

'Listen,' she threatened. 'Listen to me. If you go back to Stopton tomorrow I'll tell the police you stole the watch.'

Bill took a step back from her.

'What you talking about? What watch?'

'I saw you giving it to Marlene last night. I found it in the wall where she had hidden it and I took it back to Mrs Simpson's shop this morning.'

Bill's normal putty-coloured complexion had turned dark red.

'Marlene will be here in a second,' said Jinny, 'and she's not to know anything about this. Nothing. So listen, so that you know what to do. You've to tell Dad at tea-time, when we're all there to hear you, that you want to stay. And there's to be no more stealing, see? Not while you're here. You've to stay with Ken. In

159

the pottery with him. Be keen on pottery so that Marlene doesn't worry about you. See?'

Bill didn't answer.

'That's Marlene now,' warned Jinny. 'You know what to do. Tell them at teatime. Or I'll tell the police. And don't think I don't mean it because I do.' Jinny scrubbed at Shantih's bridle.

'He didn't half eat up that bread. I don't think you feed him proper. It's hens you feed on that old corn and he ain't no hen.'

'You can send her food parcels,' suggested Jinny.

'Eh, OK, I'll do that,' said Marlene. 'What's he been at?' she asked suspiciously, looking at Bill.

Jinny thrust a sponge into Bill's unwilling hand. 'He's helping me to clean tack,' she said and gave Bill Shantih's grass-encrusted bit to clean.

Marlene, planning ways in which they could posh up Shantih, helped Jinny to clean the saddle.

'Them old brushes don't get at the deep down dirt,' she said. 'You got to get with it. Try the Hoover on him. Or like they do with cars – a horse wash.'

'Set the table,' said Mrs Manders when they got into the house. 'What did Sue do with all her wet clothes?'

'Took them back to their tent,' said Jinny, taking knives and forks out of the drawer.

'She should have left them here,' said Mrs Manders. 'You could go over and ask her if she wants to bring them up here to dry off.'

'OK,' said Jinny. 'Though she didn't seem very keen on charity. I offered them all instant Dr Barnardo's when it rained but she didn't want it.'

'I won't see the fat horse again,' said Marlene. 'Eh, it were that podgy. What she wants to stick with that old dough ball for when she could have one like yours?'

'Bet she wouldn't change Pippen for Shantih,' said Jinny.

'Like she loves him,' said Marlene, grinning.

When she went to tell Ken and her father that their tea was ready, Jinny paused by Bill's side.

'OK?' she said. 'I mean it.' She went on to the pottery. There was only Ken there.

'Tea,' said Jinny. 'Where's Dad?'

'Bathroom,' said Ken. 'You managed it this morning?'

And Jinny told him about Shantih jumping the gate and how she had hidden the watch in among the apples.

'Marlene wants to stay,' said Jinny. 'She wants to ride Shantih. So Bill's got to stay too or she won't. If he stays, can he be with you in here? I told him that he's got to tell us at teatime that he wants to stay.'

'Does he want to?'

'He can make clay monsters,' suggested Jinny. 'That's what his comics are full of – monsters from the dawn of time, monsters from the centre of the earth, deep-sea monsters, space monsters – I had a read at some of them. Well, he can make them in clay. Be a bit of a relief seeing them solid rather than just reading about them and having them prowling round in your head.'

'If he stays,' said Ken, and suddenly he crashed his clenched fist down on the table, filling the air with white clay dust. 'The mess we've made of a kid like that! Where's he going to go? What's he going to do now? Back to Stopton with his monsters until he picks up some more of their trashy bits of obscene rubbish and then they'll shut him up and we'll all be able to forget about him.'

'Well it's not my fault,' said Jinny.

'You reckon?' said Ken. 'Not your fault?'

'Well, it's not!' repeated Jinny indignantly. 'I don't make him steal things.'

'What a nasty thought,' said Ken. 'Tuck it away out of sign. Got nothing to do with you, has it?'

'Oh, come on for tea,' said Jinny. 'I don't know what you're talking about.' She pushed the thought to the back of her mind that in any way she, Jinny Manders, might be responsible for Bill Thorpe.

Bill was sitting at the table having a pre-tea slice of bread and jam. Jinny gave him another hard look as she sat down but didn't risk saying anything more in case she aroused Marlene's suspicions.

If he didn't tell them that he wanted to stay would she phone the police? Jinny knew she wouldn't, but she knew that Bill couldn't be certain of this.

Jinny smiled at Petra, asking her when her music exam was, how long it would last, whether she would

162

need to stay overnight in Inverburgh when she sat it. When Mike put down her plate of grilled tomatoes and ham pie, Jinny thanked him sweetly. This was the way someone would behave who was the sort of person who would phone up the police and tell them that Bill had stolen the watch.

Jinny stared hard at Bill, hoping he was noticing her. They had reached the cake and second cup of tea stage. Ken had finished. Since he never ate anything that was connected with animals, not even cheese or milk or eggs, Ken's meals, mostly of raw vegetables, fruit, wholemeal bread and brown rice had their own timing, didn't fit in with the Manders' pattern of meat and veg., chips and eggs. Quite often Ken had days of not eating – to make him aware of the gift of food, he said. He was watching Jinny now, knowing that she was up to something.

Bill took his fourth piece of cake and Mrs Manders removed the plate.

'Need to leave proper early tomorrow?' asked Marlene. 'Best not sleep, eh?'

Petra said she would set her alarm, and as she always heard it, she would wake Marlene.

*But you're not going,* Jinny thought desperately and glared at Bill. She had tried kicking him under the table but had kicked Kelly instead, making the dog remove himself with wounded dignity to the far corner of the room.

*Tell them! Tell them! Go on, tell them*, Jinny thought at Bill, but Bill was stuffing the last piece of cake into his mouth.

'That policeman who was with Mrs Simpson,' Jinny said, 'does he live in Glenbost?'

'Police cottages at Ardtallon. There's two of them,' said Mr Manders.

'Could you phone him there?' asked Jinny.

'Oh yes,' said her father. 'It's really the police station.'

'Is the number in the book?' asked Jinny.

'Will be,' said Mr Manders.

'Whatever do you want to know that for?' asked Petra.

'Handy,' said Jinny. 'Handy to know.'

'What you on at?' asked Marlene suspiciously.

But Bill pushed his chair back from the table. Before he stood up he looked across at Jinny, mocking her. He knew she would never phone the police. He knew that Marlene cared more about him than learning to ride. And he knew that Jinny knew this. He wanted back to Stopton and he was going.

*Beast*, thought Jinny helplessly. *Selfish, pigging beast*.

He'd called her bluff. She wouldn't phone. There was nothing more she could do. Marlene wasn't going to get her chance to go fast like flames on Shantih. It was all hopeless.

Ken stretched out a long arm and caught Bill.

'Sit down.' said Ken. 'No hurry.' Jinny saw Ken's bony fingers biting into Bill's wrist as he forced him to sit down again.

'I was having a chat with Jinny,' said Ken, and Jinny saw the red flush creep up Bill's neck and redden his ears. He shifted uneasily in his chair.

'Jinny said she'd had a word with you.' Ken's green eyes had set as hard as stones. He forced Bill to look at him. There was no softness in Ken. He was contained in himself. Independent. Lived from his own centre. 'Jinny said you'd something to tell us.'

Everyone was looking at Ken and Bill, wondering what Ken was talking about. But no one interrupted. Not Mr Manders, or Marlene.

'Now,' said Ken, and they were all waiting for Bill to speak.

'I changed me mind,' said Bill. 'We ain't going tomorrow.'

'Oh, grand,' said Mr Manders. 'Great.'

*More food*, thought Mrs Manders and hoped that Mrs Simpson wouldn't hold the matter of the watch against her.

Marlene had sat without moving, so drawn into herself that she hardly seemed to be breathing.

'That what you really want?' she asked Bill.

'Yus,' said Bill and Marlene exploded from her chair like a rocket. Stamping her lame leg, clapping her hands, she danced round the kitchen.

'Eh, ain't that right smashing?' she cried. 'That's right proper smashing, that is! Jin's going to learn me to ride the old horse, ain't you? To sit on him proper so we can go galloping off, him and me, for miles and miles. Eh, I'm right pleased, Bill. I'm right proper pleased you want to stay!'

Jinny blew her nose hard but didn't feel so bad about it because her mother had suddenly found it necessary to start and collect up the tea plates.

'Come into the pottery, now,' said Ken, 'and I'll show you round. You can try the wheel.'

Bill went with him.

'When we going to start?' Marlene demanded.

'Ride down to Sue's,' suggested Mrs Manders. 'See if we can dry out anything for them.'

'Want me to wipe up first?' asked Marlene.

'Don't think you'd be safe,' laughed Mrs Manders.

'It's Petra's day,' said Jinny. 'We'll go and find Sue.'

'Take the old horse?'

'But of course,' said Jinny.

'Got to start and learn how to do things, ain't I? Now that I'm going to be doing the proper riding.'

# Twelve

'Give us the halter thing,' said Marlene the next morning. 'I'll do the catching bit.'

'Well, take care,' said Jinny, handing Shantih's halter to Marlene. 'Don't rush at her.'

'Eh, give over fussing. Here, how's that then?' and Marlene placed a sugar lump on the palm of her hand and tucked the halter, more or less out of sight, behind her back. 'That do? Like you showed me?'

'A scoop of nuts would be easier,' suggested Jinny. 'Then there'd be more than one mouthful. You could put her halter on while she's got her head down munching.'

'He's right fed up with all those old dried things you're always giving him. Enjoys a sugar lump he does. I've got more in me pocket.' Marlene set off confidently across the field.

Jinny watched, biting her tongue to stop herself interfering, as Marlene advanced on Shantih.

'Here you are, horse,' Marlene said and let Shantih lip up the sugar from her hand.

'Now for this rope thing. Let's be having your head down. End of that rope round your neck and that's me got you. Now this bit round your face.'

Marlene struggled to get the halter over Shantih's ears then announced triumphantly, 'That's the job,' and remembered to knot the halter rope. 'That deserves another sugar lump, that does.'

Marlene produced her bag of sugar lumps, and was just placing one correctly on her outstretched palm, when Shantih snatched it up. Without a second's hesitation, Marlene smacked Shantih hard across the muzzle. The Arab sprang back to the length of her rope, rearing away from Marlene. But Marlene hardly noticed. 'You need sorting out, you do,' she threatened darkly and turned to lead the prancing horse back to Jinny.

'D'you see that?' Marlene demanded when she reached the gate. 'Had to give him a bat on the nose.'

'I saw,' said Jinny, who had been watching helplessly. 'I told you not to hit her. She's scared of being hit because of the circus.'

'Garn,' said Marlene. 'He ain't scared. He's having you on, he is. Any road I didn't hit him, just gave him a bit bat. Cheek of him snatching at me sugar lumps.'

168

'I told you you'd be better with a scoop of nuts,' said Jinny, opening the gate, but Marlene wasn't listening.

'What's next?' she demanded. 'Going at him with the brush, ain't it? Keeping all them hairs lying nice and flat. Then on with the saddle and that's me set for the riding. 'Spect I'll be proper good today.'

An hour later Marlene wasn't feeling so confident.

'Up, down. Up, down,' chanted Jinny as she ran at Shantih's side.

'Eh, that were awful,' lamented Marlene when they stopped. 'I just go bump, bump, bump, bump. I ain't never going to be much good until I get the hang of this, am I?'

Reluctantly Jinny had to agree.

'Come on,' said Marlene. 'Let's have another bash.'

'Wait till I get my breath back,' gasped Jinny. 'Here's Sue,' she added, spotting Pippen's skewbald shape bumbling over the fields towards them. 'Perhaps Sue'll know what we're doing wrong.'

'Hullo,' said Sue, opening the gate without dismounting and riding into the field. 'You both look like the end of the world. What's wrong?'

'I'm trying to teach Marlene to post,' said Jinny. 'But I'm not doing very well.'

'Took me weeks,' said Sue.

'And me,' said Jinny, remembering the hours she had spent bumping round Major Young's paddock at the riding school in Stopton.

'Well, I ain't got weeks,' said Marlene. 'Come on. Give us another go.'

Jinny set off round the field again, holding Shantih's bridle with one hand, the other pressing Marlene's knee against the saddle and chanting, 'Up, down. Up, down,' to the rhythm of Shantih's stride, while Marlene bumped around.

'Do you want a try on Pippen?' Sue offered when they got back to her. 'He might be steadier.'

Marlene shook her head stubbornly. 'Ain't the old horse, it's me,' she said.

'Try holding on to the front of the saddle,' suggested Sue, 'and sort of push yourself up from your hands.'

Next time round Marlene tried it. She was crouched forward trying frantically to push up at the right moment when Shantih tossed her head and caught Marlene a crack on the nose.

'S'all right,' Marlene assured them, staunching the flow of blood with an inadequate paper hanky. 'I'll have it stopped in a moment. I'll not bother getting off.'

Jinny insisted that Shantih needed a rest and made Marlene dismount. Sue provided her with a bigger handkerchief.

While Marlene mopped at her nose Jinny made a hopeless face at Sue. She didn't know how else she could teach Marlene to post except by going on making Shantih trot and hoping that eventually Marlene's bumping would change into posting.

'That's it stopped,' Marlene announced, sniffing experimentally. 'Let's get back to bumping. Can't go fast, can I, until we get this up and down business right.'

They spent all afternoon in the field. Sue and Jinny taking it in turns to make Shantih trot round; but by five o'clock, although Marlene could control Shantih at a walk, her bumping was showing no signs of changing into posting.

'We'll try again tomorrow,' said Jinny. 'Shantih's had enough for today.'

Marlene didn't argue but slid obediently to the ground.

'Ain't no good, am I?' she said, looking despondently from Jinny to Sue.

'Of course you are,' cried Jinny. 'I told you, it took us ages to learn.'

'Ain't never going to learn to go fast,' despaired Marlene. 'Better go and see how Bill's doing,' she mumbled and limped quickly away from them.

'Come for a gallop on the sands,' suggested Sue when Marlene was out of sight.

Jinny hesitated, then said no, for she knew there was just a chance that Marlene might be watching from a window and would see them doing what she dreamed of doing, going fast as flames, and Jinny was beginning to think that Marlene wasn't going to manage it in the five days she had left.

Next morning Marlene brought Shantih in and groomed her before she had her breakfast.

'Give us that bit longer for bumping,' she said to Jinny.

Jinny supposed it would.

'We'll try up and down the path to the shore,' Jinny suggested after Marlene had tacked Shantih up. 'Perhaps that will be better. You'll have longer going straight. Maybe that's what was wrong yesterday, having to go round the field.'

But going along the path didn't make any difference to Marlene's bumping, it only gave Shantih more scope for sudden shies, fly canters and head tossing. By the time they had been up and down the path a few times, Jinny knew it had not been a good idea to leave the field.

'It's your fault,' she said to Shantih. 'Why can't you trot smoothly and give Marlene a chance?'

'Eh, don't be blaming the old horse.'

'Well, it is her fault,' repeated Jinny. 'We'll go back to the sea once more and then I think we'd be better in the field. And you calm down,' she added severely to Shantih.

'Ready? Off we go. Up, down. Up, down.'

Jinny had knotted a rope to the bit ring to make leading Shantih easier and when her horse shied at absolutely nothing at all she tugged at the rope, spoke sharply to her, feeling as irritated with her as she had with Bramble when he was having one of his spooky days. Normally Shantih could do no wrong in Jinny's eyes. On the surface she was annoyed when the Arab misbehaved, rearing or bucking her off, but underneath Jinny thought up excuses for her wild behaviour, and loved her so much that it didn't really matter to Jinny how wild she was. But now Jinny was thinking about Marlene, desperately wanting her to be able to ride before she had to go back to Stopton, and so much depended on Shantih.

'Trot on,' said Jinny crossly as Shantih flung herself sideways in a sudden canter. 'How is Marlene ever going to learn to post if you go on mucking about all the time?' She gave Shantih's rope another sharp tug.

'Up, down. Up, down,' Jinny chanted as they trotted back to Finmory.

Sue rode up later in the morning to find Jinny holding a glooming Shantih while Marlene pressed a paper hanky to her bleeding nose.

'Knew you needed me,' said Sue, handing up a larger handkerchief. 'What happened?'

'Same thing,' said Jinny. 'And Marlene was nearly posting, weren't you?'

'No,' said Marlene from behind Sue's handkerchief. 'I were just at me bumping.'

'Well, you might have been posting in a minute,' snapped Jinny, 'if she'd been a bit more sensible. You idiot horse.'

The Arab swung away from Jinny, her ears pinned back, her eyes rolling, as she pawed at the ground with a front hoof.

'Behave yourself,' Jinny told her. 'You think you can do what you like, don't you?'

Shantih tossed her head, jangling the bit and narrowly missed hitting Marlene in the face for a third time.

'If I were you,' said Sue, 'I'd ride her in a martingale.'

'I did,' said Jinny. 'When I had one. Clare Burnley lent me one. She was better behaved with it on. It stopped her getting her head up.'

'Why don't you buy one? Can't be very expensive.'

Jinny thought of the money in her tin box, of the lungeing rein she was going to buy with it. She saw herself standing in the middle of the field and Shantih cantering smoothly round on the end of her new lungeing rein.

'Don't think I could afford a martingale,' said Jinny.

'Pity,' said Sue. 'I don't think Shantih tossing her head up the way she does helps Marlene to post. And it would stop her rearing with you.'

Jinny groaned inwardly. If Marlene was ever going to go fast, she would have to control Shantih by herself and it certainly wouldn't help her if Shantih reared.

'Oh well,' said Jinny, reluctantly abandoning the dream of the lungeing rein. 'I suppose I could sell a few of my drawings.'

'Would we need to go into Inverburgh to buy it?' Sue asked.

'Yes,' said Jinny brightening at the thought. It was going to be a very hot afternoon and she was beginning to be a bit fed up with running beside Shantih, chanting her "up, down," refrain. 'Might as well go this afternoon. If I can persuade Dad to run us to the main road we could catch a bus at two o'clock and there's one back at six.'

Marlene said she would stay with the old horse and Jinny said she most certainly would not.

'Got to practise,' Marlene insisted. 'Ain't got much time left.'

'We'll practise again this evening,' Jinny promised. 'And then we'll have a martingale and you can hold on to the neck strap.'

'What?' said Marlene. Then, giving her nose a final dab, decided that it didn't really concern her. 'Just have one more bump round the field,' she said and gathered up Shantih's reins.

Jinny left Sue and Marlene to take off Shantih's tack and went in search of her father.

'Could you run us in for the two o'clock bus?' she asked.

Her father said he would and Jinny climbed up to her bedroom and reluctantly chose six drawings to take to Nell Storr. They had to be good ones. Nell knew the difference.

Jinny put the six drawings in a brown envelope and laid it carefully on her bed. She took down the cash box, pulled off the sellotape and took out the five one pound notes that were left in it. It didn't look much for months of saving, but Jinny had had to pay for Shantih's shoeing which had used up quite a lot of the money that Nell Storr had paid for her drawings.

*A pound each for six drawings,* Jinny thought. *That's six pounds and five, that's eleven pounds. That should be plenty for a martingale.*

Standing in her bedroom, eleven pounds had seemed hordes of money, but somehow, as they stood looking in the window of the saddler's shop, it didn't seem quite so much.

'Pretty expensive-looking,' said Sue doubtfully.

Jinny agreed, but as far as she knew it was the only saddlers in Inverburgh.

'Should we go and sell your drawings first?' Sue asked.

'Let's find out how much a martingale will cost,' said Jinny. 'Perhaps I'll not need to sell them.'

'Come on then,' nagged Marlene. 'We going in then? Got to have plenty time to pick a present for me mum. She likes something real nice does me mum. Proper fussy she is.'

Jinny scowled at Marlene. At that particular moment she couldn't have cared less how fussy Mrs Thorpe was.

'Shall I lead the way, seeing you're a bit shy like,' said Marlene, pushing open the saddler's door. Jinny and Sue followed after her.

'Can I assist?' asked a slim young man, emerging from behind a glass counter.

Jinny was gazing entranced at saddles and bridles, horse rugs and numnahs, black jackets and breeches, and, best of all, hanging in a corner, a bunch of lungeing reins.

'We want to buy a what-do-you-call-it,' said Marlene. 'One of them things to stop me bumping.'

The young man raised elegant eyebrows.

'We want to know how much a standing martingale would cost,' said Jinny quickly.

'Pony size?'

'Arab size,' said Jinny.

The assistant brought a standing martingale and laid it on the glass counter.

'Six pounds fifty,' he said.

'Eh!' exclaimed Marlene. 'For a bit belt!'

'We'll come back later,' said Jinny.

'Certainly, madam,' said the assistant, putting away the martingale.

'Nell Storr's,' said Jinny when they were out of the shop.

'Best be quick,' said Marlene. 'I've got to pick me mum's pressie.'

But Nell Storr wasn't in her craft shop. She was

away for a week. The girl behind the counter offered to keep Jinny's drawings until Nell came back but said that only Nell herself could pay Jinny for them, so Jinny said that was no good and kept her drawings.

Jinny stared gloomily across the road. Now that she couldn't afford to buy it a martingale seemed the most important thing in the world; the only thing that could ever teach Marlene to post.

'If we'd known I could have lent you the money,' said Sue.

'Well, we didn't know, did we?' snapped Jinny.

'It don't matter,' said Marlene. 'Bloomin' well too much money. I'll just look for something for me mum and then we'll get back to me trotting.'

'How about something from Nell's?' suggested Jinny.

Marlene regarded the pottery, glass, wood carvings and woven goods that filled the craft shop window.

'Naw,' she said disdainfully. 'Me mum likes pretty things, not that junk.'

An hour and six ice creams later, Marlene found a pawn shop.

'Eh, we'll get something here,' she cried. 'People have to pop right pretty things sometimes.'

The dirty window was filled with old clothes, watches, vases, jewellery, ornaments and all the other belongings that people had brought to the pawn shop, borrowed money on and never bothered to buy back.

'That's proper pretty,' said Marlene, pointing to a small china posy of flowers. 'She'd fancy that.'

Jinny and Sue followed Marlene into the pawn shop. Jinny looked round curiously at the clutter of abandoned possessions.

'It's all rubbish,' said Sue.

Jinny nodded but she supposed that all the things her family owned would look much the same if you brought them here.

Marlene bought her posy bowl from a toothless young woman.

'Right bargain for fifty pence,' she said, carrying it proudly out of the shop.

'It's a bit dirty,' said Sue.

'Give it a right scrub up and it'll be real nice. Bet you'd have paid five pounds for it in one of your fancy shops. Saw one of those things we were going to buy. Be cheaper in there.'

'What things?' said Jinny. 'A martingale? In there?'

'Don't believe you,' said Sue flatly. 'You wouldn't know what a martingale looked like.'

'Just seen one, ain't I? Come in and I'll show you.'

'Let's see that leather belt thing,' Marlene said, pointing it out to the woman in the pawn shop.

'Would it be this you're meaning?' the woman said and laid a standing martingale on the counter.

'Wherever did that come from?' Jinny demanded in amazement.

'Came with a job lot from a sale,' said the woman. 'Lot of old junk out of the stables. Had to take it to get a chest our Jim had his eye on.'

'It's not really a martingale,' said Sue critically. 'Only a bit of one. Someone's made up the neck strap from two stirrup leathers.'

'Oh, but it would do,' gasped Jinny. 'It would be fine. How much is it?'

'One pound and fifty pence,' said the woman. 'Beautiful leather, it is.'

Jinny still hadn't recovered from her surprise by the time she was standing in the stable fitting the martingale round Shantih's neck. She had cleaned it thoroughly and it seemed perfectly good. It was, thought Jinny, a bargain.

'Eh, this is it, ain't it?' said Marlene, as Jinny led Shantih down to the field. 'I'll be able to do the up and down now, won't it?'

'At least she'll not be able to bash you on the nose,' said Jinny, tightening Shantih's girth and holding her while Marlene mounted. 'Walk her to the hedge and back by yourself and then we'll trot.'

Jinny watched as Marlene rode Shantih away from her. She sat very straight in the saddle. Jinny's hard hat firmly on her head, her heels pressed down, her elbows tucked in. Marlene was in charge of Shantih. She wasn't going to let any old horse boss her.

When they reached the hedge and Marlene turned

back to Jinny. Shantih broke into a jog. Instantly, Marlene had checked her and brought her back to a walk.

'Grab hold,' said Marlene to Jinny, 'and off we go.'

But by the time they were halfway round the field both girls knew that the martingale wasn't going to work a miracle with Marlene's posting. Clutching the neck strap, she continued to bump.

As they walked back to Finmory through the summer dusk Marlene said. 'It's me leg, ain't it? I ain't ever going to be able to do anything but bump.'

'Don't be daft,' said Jinny loudly, because she had been thinking the same thing herself. 'Of course you'll be able to post. It takes time to learn, that's all. Of course you'll be able to do it.'

'Some hopes,' said Marlene.

'And you're doing really well controlling her and riding her.'

'Riding?' exclaimed Marlene in disgust. 'You can't ride when all the old horse is doing is crawling round. I don't call that riding, I don't.'

They weren't any more successful the next morning, although both Sue and Jinny had spent all morning making Shantih trot round the field. Marlene went on bumping.

'While we're getting our breath back,' said Sue, 'try standing up in your stirrups.'

Marlene did so.

'Now sit down and stand up. Go on, do it several times.'

'Now,' instructed Sue, 'don't sit down in between, hardly touch your seat onto the saddle and stand up again quickly.'

Marlene tried but each time she sat down with a flop and had to reorganise herself into standing up.

'Don't sit down,' said Jinny. 'That's why you get bumped.'

'Can't help it,' said Marlene. 'I ain't trying to get bumped am I?'

Ken appeared at the field gate.

'Eh,' cried Marlene, all her attention riveted on Ken, 'he ain't got our Bill with him.' She swung Shantih round and urged her to the gate.

'Where's our Bill?' Marlene shouted as Shantih trotted forward.

'Make her walk,' yelled Jinny as Marlene bumped precariously from side to side.

And then, to Jinny's and Sue's delight, Marlene was posting. She went up too far and came down with a flop but she was most definitely and decidedly posting.

'She's done it,' cried Sue.

'Look at me,' Marlene yelled. 'I'm trotting proper. I can do it!'

Sue on Pippen led the way round the field and Marlene trotted behind her, posting most of the way. She returned to the gate, her face glowing scarlet with effort and success.

'Couldn't do it before,' Marlene told Ken. 'Right down in the dumps I was. Thought it were me leg mucking things up. Here, I'll do it again. Just you watch me.'

Marlene and Sue trotted round again. This time Marlene posted all the way.

'How were that?' she demanded triumphantly. 'I'm doing proper good now, ain't I?'

'Nearly as good as Bill and his pots,' said Ken. 'Come into the pottery after lunch and he'll give you a demo.'

Marlene clapped her hand to her mouth.

'He went right out of me head with all that posting,' she admitted.

Sue stayed for lunch and afterwards they went into the pottery.

'Bit squint, that one,' said Marlene, looking critically at Bill's pots.

'Ain't easy,' said Bill. 'Watch this.' He sat down at the wheel and began to shape a pot out of a lump of wet clay.

'How's that?' he asked when he had finished.

'Smashing,' said Jinny. 'You've learned jolly quickly.'

'Our Bill was looking right pleased, did you notice?' Marlene asked as they went back to the field.

Jinny said she had.

'You sit there and watch us,' Marlene said as she mounted Shantih. 'Sue and me'll have a bit trot round.'

Jinny sat on the gate and watched as Marlene trotted round the field behind Sue. There was no doubt about it, Marlene had learned to post.

'Shall we have another go after tea?' suggested Marlene when Sue said it was five o'clock and she would have to go.

'No,' said Jinny. 'Shantih's had enough for one day.'

'Tomorrow then,' said Marlene, dismounting.

Jinny took Shantih's reins, rubbed her hand down her horse's neck, straightening her mane, said, 'Yes. Tomorrow.' Then she took Shantih into the stable while Marlene went to see how Bill's potting was getting on.

'You're being very well behaved,' Jinny said to Shantih as she watched the Arab eating a small feed of oats and nuts. It might be the martingale that was stopping Shantih rearing, but in the whole afternoon of walking and trotting about the field Shantih had only bucked once.

'Expect you like having Pippen for company,' said Jinny, but she knew that it couldn't only be that. Shantih had often had the Highland ponies with her when Jinny had been trying to school her before. Reluctantly Jinny had to admit to herself that it must be something to do with Marlene. It wasn't that Marlene knew anything at all about how to treat horses, just that when her mind was set on a thing there was no room in it for anything else. When Shantih had tried to buck, Marlene had slapped her hard on the shoulder and told Shantih to stop his old nonsense, that if he started that mucking about she'd be bumping again. Shantih had given another protesting hitch of her quarters and trotted on.

They all spent the next afternoon on the shore. Mr and Mrs Manders, Mike and Petra, Ken and Bill, brought down a picnic. Sue's parents joined them. Jinny spent her time keeping an eye on Marlene and Shantih, watching anxiously as Marlene rode Shantih about. Tomorrow was Friday and then Saturday, when Marlene and Bill would go home to Stopton. Jinny didn't want anything to happen to spoil Marlene's confidence before that.

The afterglow of sunset turned sky, sea and wet sands into a glowing sapphire. *We must be breathing blue air*, Jinny thought. Sue and Marlene were walking the horses at the water's edge and the spray from their horses' hooves glittered ice blue, diamond, aquamarine. They were held in a jewelled paperweight of sky and sea.

'Home,' said Mrs Manders, beginning to gather up the remains of the picnic, and arranging with the Hortons to come up for supper on Saturday evening.

*Marlene will be in Stopton then*, Jinny thought. *Everything will be the same for us, but not for her.*

Mr and Mrs Horton began to walk back to their tent. Jinny's family, Ken and Bill, wandered raggedly back to Finmory.

'Don't be long,' Mrs Horton called to Sue.

'Coming now,' replied Sue and turned Pippen to follow her parents. Shantih went with Pippen. Jinny ran over the sands towards them, took Shantih's bridle to turn her back to Finmory.

'Eh, let's go with them,' pleaded Marlene. 'Just along a bit and then I can have a last trot back.'

'OK,' said Jinny and walked between the two horses. She felt soaked through with the day's sunlight, warm and contented. She glanced at Marlene sitting very correctly on Shantih and thought that tomorrow Marlene could have a canter. If Sue rode with her, Shantih would behave, would stop when Pippen stopped. Jinny thought Marlene would manage.

Sue rode off to her tent and Marlene turned Shantih round and began to trot back. Jinny ran beside them.

'Got the knack of that posting now, ain't I?' Marlene asked as they walked up the path to Finmory.

Jinny agreed that she most certainly had.

'Reckon I'm good enough now, ain't I?' demanded Marlene.

There was a tense, strained quality in her voice that made Jinny look up at her.

'Good enough for what?' asked Jinny.

'You know,' said Marlene. 'To go fast.'

'Yes,' said Jinny. 'You can have a canter with Sue tomorrow. I was thinking about it. There's a good canter on the moors. We can go up there tomorrow. I'll

186

wait at the end and you and Sue can gallop up to me. Shantih's bound to stop. She knows that bit. She'll stop when she reaches me.'

'Eh no!' exclaimed Marlene. 'I don't want you lot there. Just me and the old horse, that's what I mean.'

'But you can't,' said Jinny. 'You couldn't manage Shantih by yourself.'

'I could that. We get on right good. I don't put up with none of that nonsense you have.'

'Yes, but . . .' began Jinny, then changed what she had been going to say into, 'we'll see tomorrow.'

She didn't think she could possibly explain to Marlene the difference between riding Shantih on her own and riding Shantih with herself and Sue looking after her.

*Really Marlene knows nothing about controlling horses. Most of the time she doesn't even notice what Shantih's doing,* Jinny thought.

'That's fixed up about me riding,' Marlene said, before she went to bed. 'I'll take him down to the sands and have a bit ride on him tomorrow, by myself. That's it, ain't it?' and she was through the door before Jinny had time to protest.

'Could she manage Shantih by herself?' asked Mike doubtfully.

'Of course not,' said Jinny. ' 'Course she couldn't. She's just talking nonsense. Of course I shan't let her gallop Shantih by herself.'

# Thirteen

In her dream, Jinny was running through Stopton streets, chasing Marlene and Shantih. The faster Jinny ran, the faster Marlene galloped Shantih away from her. 'Stop!' Jinny screamed. 'Stop! She's mine!' But Marlene only laughed and rode faster than ever between the roaring traffic. 'Stop!' screamed Jinny again and woke herself back into her own bed at Finmory.

She lay, the dream still vivid in her mind. It was daylight, early morning blue. Jinny got up and looked out of the window to make sure that Shantih was still in her field.

The Arab was grazing peacefully by the far hedge. Being herself in the field, untroubled by humans. Perhaps Ken was right, Jinny thought, when he said that horses should be left alone to be horses; that they didn't need humans to ride them.

Shantih flicked her tail, lifted each foot in slow, deliberate steps as she grazed along the hedgerow. Jinny hesitated, unwilling to break into the secret horse world in which Shantih moved. Not calling her name, not yet, but knowing that in a minute or two she would, just for the joy of seeing Shantih look up and know her.

But before Jinny had time to open the window and call down to her horse, something startled Shantih. She jerked her head up, ears pricked, neck arched. From her window, Jinny couldn't see anything that might have disturbed her. She thought that it might be Ken and Kelly out for an early morning walk, or Mr MacKenzie taking a shortcut down to his fields by the sea.

Then Jinny saw who it was. Marlene was standing at the field gate. She had Jinny's hard hat on her head, Shantih's halter in one hand and a sugar lump on the other.

*Well*, thought Jinny, *of all the cheek. She's going to ride my horse. Good job I saw her.*

Jinny lifted her hand to open the window, to shout at Marlene and tell her to leave Shantih alone; but somehow she couldn't do it. She watched as Marlene limped across the field, saw Shantih take a few strides towards her, then wait. Marlene fumbled with sugar lumps and halter and although Jinny couldn't hear her she could see her mouth moving as she talked to the horse.

Confidently, Marlene led Shantih back to the gate, manoeuvred her through it and closed it behind them. Shantih pranced at the end of her halter rope, fretting to reach the stable, but Marlene paid no attention to her impatience. She checked that the gate was shut and then led Shantih out of sight.

*I'll go down to the stables*, Jinny thought, scrambling into her clothes. *Stop her there. Go with her if she wants to ride.*

Jinny ran lightly through the garden and down to the stables. She hesitated at the stable doorway. Inside she could hear the sounds of Marlene grooming Shantih.

'Come on, now. Stand still when I'm brushing you. Got to get you right shiny. Can't have you looking a mess. Not when we're going galloping. Got to be all sparkling, you have.'

*Go in and stop her*, Jinny told herself. *You know she can't manage Shantih. She could fall, jam her foot in a stirrup, be dragged. If Shantih got a fright, Marlene wouldn't know what to do. Anything, anything could happen to them. She doesn't mean to go back to the field.*

Jinny knew quite certainly where Marlene meant to ride. She was going to take Shantih down to the shore and gallop her over the sands.

*She won't be able to control her*, Jinny thought. *Won't be able to stop her.* For Jinny knew how

Shantih could become so excited that unless you stopped her she would go plunging over the boulders that made a barrier between the fields and the sand. To cross them safely you had to bring your horse to a slow walk. Even to trot through them was dangerous.

*Go on in and stop her*, Jinny told herself.

But Jinny couldn't; couldn't make herself march into the stable and spoil everything for Marlene.

Jinny knew that it was what she would have wanted to do if she had been Marlene. If she had had to leave Shantih tomorrow and go back to Stopton, Jinny would have wanted to gallop by herself over the sands of Finmory Bay; to be alone with Shantih, sharing the ecstasy of galloping together – the freedom, the joy. To hoard the moments in her mind so that she would always have them there, to bring them out, to re-live them during the black times.

'Eh, you look proper nice,' Marlene told Shantih. 'Now for your bridle and the martingale thing. Watch that big tongue of yours, I ain't made for licking. You put this in your mouth, that'll sort you out.'

But if Marlene fell off . . . if Shantih hurt herself . . . Jinny had to stop her, couldn't take the risk of letting Marlene harm Shantih.

Jinny took a step towards the stable door. She had to go in, had to stop her. *Be sensible. Be responsible*, she told herself. *You know best.*

Marlene's white, pinched face swam into the front

191

of Jinny's mind, as she had seen it reflected in the shop mirror, as she had looked when she had realised that Jinny knew the truth about Bill.

And Jinny knew that she couldn't do it. She couldn't bear to stop Marlene, couldn't bear to go into the stable and spoil it all.

*But Shantih* . . . thought Jinny, yet it made no difference.

'Now your saddle,' said Marlene. 'And heave ho the old belly band.'

Jinny bit hard on the knuckles of her clenched fist, flung herself away from the stables, left Shantih to Marlene, and went running as fast as she could through the garden and up the hillside behind Finmory.

Not looking back, Jinny climbed steadily until she was sure that she was high enough up to be able to see the sands and the path leading down to the bay. Then she turned, crouched down by a boulder and picked out the grey stone stable buildings.

Marlene was leading Shantih into the yard. They were tiny, puppet figures – a girl with a lame leg and a chestnut Arab, her mane and tail blown out by the breeze, lifting her white legs impatiently high as she danced out of the dark stable doorway into the sunlit yard.

Three times Marlene tried to scramble up into the saddle and three times Shantih sprang away from her.

'Don't hold the reins so tight,' Jinny said. She itched to be there in the yard, to put out her hand and hold Shantih still for Marlene. 'Don't dig your toe into her side.'

Then, at her fourth attempt, Marlene made it, and was sitting in the saddle, while Shantih plunged forward and trotted down the path to the sea.

A kind of stillness came over Jinny as she sat, remote and high, crouching by the boulders, her eyes held to the figures of the girl and the horse. No matter what happened Jinny couldn't have taken her eyes away from them. If Shantih went mad, raced, runaway crazy over the sands, Jinny had to watch it happening. By turning away from the stable doorway, she had said, 'Yes'. Had allowed this to happen and now she could only watch. Had to watch.

Shantih went trotting out, her neck arched, the sea breeze winnowing her mane, her white hooves flashing over the short grass. Marlene sat posting diligently, sitting very upright, looking straight ahead. When they reached the ridge of boulders. Marlene steadied Shantih to a walk and she picked her way through them, clipping and stumbling in her haste to reach the shore.

Then they were on the sands. Shantih gave a half rear, leapt forward and raced away. She stretched her neck low, thundered the beat of her hooves against the glimmering drum skin of the wet sands. The track of her hoofprints flared out behind her.

For a minute Marlene lost her balance, was thrown forward over Shantih's withers but somehow, her hands grabbing at the neck strap, her knees held against the knee rolls, her feet wedged crookedly in the stirrups, she stayed in the saddle.

And although Marlene was still crouched over Shantih's neck Jinny knew that she wasn't going to come off. She had found her balance against the speed of the horse. Her hands low on Shantih's neck, her knees pressed into the knee rolls, Marlene was looking straight ahead as Shantih stormed the white brilliance of sea dazzle and gleaming sands. They went like flames, the flickering, burning, chestnut mare and the brightness of her rider laughing aloud into the silence of the morning. No longer lame.

As the Arab flew over the beach towards the first black shards of rock at the far side of the bay, Marlene was completely out of control. Tight as a limpet she clung on to the horse's back as they swerved between the rocks.

When they reached the cliffs and Shantih could gallop no further, she skidded to a violent halt, flung up her head and in a split second had plunged round and was galloping back across the sands to Finmory. Marlene lost a stirrup, slipped dangerously to one side but somehow managed to stop herself falling off. In one hand she clutched reins, martingale and a lump of mane, while her other hand was clenched on to the pommel of the saddle. She was crouched over Shantih's withers but her eyes were bright with excitement and her face open and laughing with sheer delight.

Yet still Jinny didn't move. She sat hardly breathing, her long hair shielding her expressionless face as she watched this stranger riding her horse.

Before they reached the barricade of smooth pebbles Shantih broke into a ragged trot. She clattered her way through the stones at a walk and Marlene was able to push herself upright in the saddle. She found her stirrup and fumbled to reorganise the lassos of reins, so that by the time they reached the path Marlene was in control again.

Alert and gay, Shantih trotted back to Finmory. Marlene posted. She had done what she had set out to do. Not once did Marlene look back at the sea.

Jinny saw Marlene reach the stableyard, drop down from Shantih and take her back out of the sun through the dark doorway.

Jinny had no words for it but she knew that something had changed. By her own choice she had let Marlene ride Shantih, had shared with this girl, whom she hadn't liked much, her most secret possession – what it was like to gallop alone on Shantih. The part of Jinny that clutched tight and hard on to anything that belonged to her had released its hold, just a little bit. She jumped up from the hillside, stretching her cramped legs as she went leaping down the hill. Her hair blew out behind her, her feet found their own way. Her arms outstretched to keep her balance, Jinny half ran, half flew down to Shantih and Marlene.

By the time Jinny reached the stable Marlene had taken Shantih's tack off and was leading her out to her field.

'You just up?' she asked Jinny.

'More or less,' said Jinny.

'Eh, we'd a right proper ride. It were real great it were. Me and the old horse, just us two on the beach. And whee! We didn't half gallop.'

'Good,' said Jinny. 'I'm glad.' And she meant it.

Later in the day when Jinny asked Marlene if she wanted to ride Shantih in the field, Marlene shook her head.

'Ain't got time,' she said. 'Got me packing to do.'

'Don't be daft,' said Jinny. 'All you've got is that tartan shopper and that's been packed all the time you've been here.'

Marlene grinned. 'Got to be ready,' she said.

'Don't you want another ride?'

'Naw,' said Marlene. 'I can ride now, don't need no more learning, do I? I got me own things to see to.'

In the afternoon Marlene checked to see that Bill was still working in the pottery, then went off by herself. Jinny didn't see her again until teatime.

'Where were you?' Jinny asked her. 'I couldn't find you anywhere. Sue's mother was teaching me how to play the guitar but there's not much hope. I can't hear the difference in the notes. What were you doing?'

'Minding me own business,' said Marlene. 'But I'll show you when I've got it fixed up.'

The evening was overlapping, evanescent shades of grey, the sea a distant snail trail glimmer, the last of the day drained out of the sky. Jinny was sprawled in an armchair, half reading a book, half holding back the thought that first thing tomorrow Bill and Marlene would be going back to Stopton.

'Psst!' said Marlene, appearing at the side of Jinny's chair. 'Come on out with me. I've got something to show you.'

'It's nearly dark,' said Jinny. 'Can't you show me here?'

'Got me mum's torch,' said Marlene. 'Come on.'

Jinny followed her out to the stables.

'Now,' said Marlene, opening up the plastic carrier she had been holding. 'Listen right careful so you understand.' She emptied twenty or thirty small knobbly parcels on to the tack room table.

'What on earth are they?' demanded Jinny.

'Sugar lumps, of course,' said Marlene. 'For the old horse. To say thank you, like. He can't half gallop, he can't. Eh . . .' Marlene's black eyes sparkled in the torchlight as the thrill of her morning's gallop filled her memory. 'It were right proper good. Now you listen careful. I've done them up for him. One for each week. Don't want him having rotten teeth.'

'Is that where you were this afternoon?' Jinny asked. 'Buying these?'

'At Mrs Simpson's. She gave me a right sinker, she did.' Marlene arranged the bags in rows. 'Last him for ages, them will. Come on and we'll give him one lot now.'

The torch turned the grey light into darkness so Marlene switched it off, and they walked together to where Shantih waited by the gate.

'That's your lot,' Marlene said when Shantih had crunched her way through the last sugar lump. 'Bet you don't meet anyone as soft as me for all the rest of your life. This has been your lucky summer, this has.'

Jinny heard the catch in Marlene's voice, heard her swallow hard.

'You'll come back,' stated Jinny.

'No chance,' said Marlene.

She laid her hand with its bitten nails against Shantih's flat-boned cheek, straightened the silky fineness of Shantih's forelock, and held out her hand letting Shantih lip at her palm.

'You ain't a bad old horse,' she said, and with a last rub at Shantih's velvet muzzle, Marlene left her and walked back to Finmory.

'But of course you'll come back,' insisted Jinny.

'I'm only here with Bill. We won't neither of us be back.'

'You'll come back even if Bill doesn't want to. We

want you to come back. Dad will write to your parents. Next Easter or next summer, you'll see.'

But there was a hollowness about Jinny's assurances. They both knew it couldn't be certain. Marlene would go back to Stopton tomorrow and probably they would never see each other again.

They stopped outside the back door. Marlene looked round the darkening garden and up to the high reaches of the moor.

'You ain't half spoilt, you ain't. Having all this.'

'I know,' said Jinny.

'It's not the horse, or living here. I'd be right bored here after a bit. Like me fish and chips, I do. It's your family. Your Mike, he ain't never going to go pinching stuff. And your Dad, he doesn't go off much does he?'

'No,' said Jinny, and she struggled to find words to tell Marlene that she knew how spoilt she was; knew she had far too much, but just now there was nothing she could do about it. She had to go on being Jinny Manders.

Suddenly Jinny grabbed Marlene's hand.

'Come on,' she said, hurrying her indoors and up to her room.

For a second Jinny stood staring at her competition painting, trying to fix it for ever in her mind's eye. It was only about six months since Jinny had painted it but already Shantih had changed. When Jinny had drawn her for the painting she had been wild and free, roaming over the moors, part of the freedom. Now she shared her life with humans. Answered to her name. Knew Jinny.

Very carefully Jinny unpinned the picture. She rolled it up quickly, found the cardboard tube in which the magazine had returned it to her, and fitted her painting into it.

'It's your share in Shantih,' said Jinny, holding the painting out to Marlene. 'Your share in Finmory for always.'

'That's your good painting,' said Marlene. 'I can't take that. It ain't right.'

'Please,' said Jinny desperately. 'Please. It's the best I've got.'

Marlene hesitated, then took it from Jinny. 'Thanks,' she said. 'I'll keep it proper careful. Always.'

Next morning Mr Manders drove Bill, Marlene, Ken and Jinny into Inverburgh in time for the Stopton train. In the station buffet they made stiff polite noises at each other, Mr Manders assuring the Thorpes that they must come back to Finmory whenever they wanted to. Any time during the school holidays, they had only to phone him and he'd meet them at Inverburgh. In the draughty, echoing, morning station, waiting for the hands of the station clock to jerk round to the figures that would let Mr Manders say, 'Better be getting onto the platform,' it sounded to Jinny more unlikely than ever that Marlene would come back to Finmory.

'Back to the la-di-dahs,' said Marlene, mocking them. She was clutching her tartan shopper, thinking about Stopton. 'Been proper posh staying with you lot it has.'

Marlene handed the ticket collector the two tickets she had been holding in her hand since they left Finmory. She went first through the barrier.

Bill nudged Jinny. 'Here,' he said. 'I left something for you with Ken.' He followed his sister onto the platform.

'I am not crying,' said Jinny as they drove back to Finmory because both Ken and her father couldn't possibly not have noticed that she was. She had reached the red-eyed, gulping stage.

'Bill made a mug for you,' said Ken.

'He told me,' said Jinny.

'He was really keen on the pottery once he got going,' said Mr Manders.

'Gave him the address of a mate of mine who has a pottery in Stopton,' said Ken. 'I'll phone him up in a week or so and if Bill hasn't got in touch with him, he'll look Bill up. See he gets going on with it.'

'A chance for him?' said Mr Manders hopefully.

'A chance,' said Ken.

'But Marlene,' said Jinny. 'Why should she have to go back to Stopton?'

'Because she wants to,' said Ken. 'Her whole life is there. All the people she loves. She's OK, is Marlene.'

'Tough as old boots,' smiled Mr Manders.

But Jinny didn't think she was, not underneath. She remembered something she had heard Ken say once – the skin beneath the skull.

Mrs Manders was baking when they got back to Finmory.

'Run over to the farm and see if Mrs MacKenzie can give you some eggs,' she said to Jinny, and without even bothering to protest that Mike and Petra could have gone, Jinny took the money and went.

She caught Shantih, put her bridle on, and rode bareback along the track to the farm. It was odd to be riding without Marlene. She felt cold and empty inside, strangely lost without Marlene's company.

Why had Marlene had to go back to Stopton? Why couldn't she have stayed at Finmory, shared Jinny's family? Why couldn't it be like that? Jinny thought bitterly.

But she knew it would have been no use. Ken had been right. The people Marlene loved were all in Stopton and Marlene had to be with them.

Round a bend in the track came Mr MacKenzie, driving his tractor. Jinny felt Shantih stiffen, and drop behind her bit as the tractor snorted and clattered towards them.

'Get on old horse! None of that nonsense,' Jinny said, and she slapped Shantih hard on the shoulder.

'You're not to go jumping my gates,' Mr MacKenzie

shouted at her. 'Now I'm warning you, lass, I'll not be having it.'

'It was an emergency,' Jinny shouted back.

'Well, don't be having another one.'

'I won't,' said Jinny and rode on.

Then suddenly she realised that Shantih had passed the tractor without bucking or rearing. Her mouth spread into a wide grin, for that was exactly how Marlene would have ridden past the tractor, her mind fixed on where she was going, looking straight ahead.

'Eh,' praised Jinny, clapping Shantih's neck, 'that were proper good, that were.'

*I'll write and tell Marlene,* Jinny thought. *Tell her that she's taught me to ride.* And Jinny flicked her hair back behind her ears, deciding to go and find Sue after she had got the eggs.

*Forward the eggs,* thought Jinny, and laughed. There were weeks and weeks of holiday still ahead of her and Sue to ride with.

'Be right proper good,' she said aloud. 'Be right proper good, eh, old horse?' and Jinny let Shantih canter on through the bright morning.

# EDITOR'S NOTE

Humans have been falling in love with horses for centuries – Jinny and Shantih, created in the 1970s are relative newcomers to the scene.

Here at Catnip we feel that this series was ahead of its time and is as fresh and relevant today as when it was first published. For this reason we have left Patricia Leitch's text in its original, startlingly beautiful, form.

Some of the cultural references reflect the time in which the books were written: a new martingale costs only six pounds fifty; Jinny imagines riding with Princess Anne in the Olympic team, whereas today she would be more likely to be teammates with Zara Phillips, Princess Anne's daughter. Yet the social issues and emotions tackled in each book are as timeless as the spiritual bond between girl and horse.

# For Love of a Horse

## Patricia Leitch

*The horse was a pure-bred Arab. She came,
bright and dancing, flaunting into the ring,
her tail held high over her quarters, her silken
mane flowing over the crest of her neck.*

When Jinny Manders moves to wilds of
Finmory in the Scottish Highlands she has
only one dream: a pony of her own. That's
until a near-wild chestnut Arab steals her heart.
But it seems the mare will never trust her,
even though Jinny would risk everything
to save the horse she loves.

# A Devil to Ride

## Patricia Leitch

*Shantih bucked again; heels flung skywards, head and neck disappearing from in front of Jinny as she went soaring through the air, her long, straight, red-gold hair flying out behind her.*

Worried that someone will discover that Shantih is too wild for her to ride, Jinny is desperate for help. When star showjumper Clare Burnley comes to the moors, Jinny thinks her prayers have been answered. But Clare's help comes at a price – one that Jinny seems only too willing to pay.

You can find out more about other exciting Catnip books by visiting:

www.catnippublishing.co.uk